OVERLAND

ALSO BY
YASMIN CORDERY KHAN

Edgware Road

OVERLAND

YASMIN CORDERY KHAN

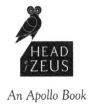

An Apollo Book

First published in the United Kingdom in 2024 by Head of Zeus,
part of Bloomsbury Publishing Plc

9 7 5 3 1 2 4 6 8

A catalogue record for this book is available from the British Library.

ISBN (HB): 9781801107389
ISBN (XTPB): 9781801107396
ISBN (E): 9781801107419

Cover design: Simon Michele

Printed and bound in Great Britain by
CPI Group (UK) Ltd, Croydon CR0 4YY

MIX
Paper | Supporting
responsible forestry
FSC
www.fsc.org   FSC® C013604

Head of Zeus
First Floor East
5–8 Hardwick Street
London EC1R 4RG

WWW.HEADOFZEUS.COM

The information in this book is as reliable as I can make it; as I've just mentioned, some of it is liable to change, rather abruptly. At the same time, some of the things I may mention as impossible, like restrictions on entering certain countries, can be overcome by persistent individuals.

Douglas Brown, *Overland to India: A Practical Guide to Getting There Through Istanbul, Turkey, Iran, Afghanistan and West Pakistan Cheaply, Happily and Unhassled*, 1971

PART 1

DOVER

The world was his oyster. That's what disappointed me about dear Fred, you know? The tabloids printed the scandal about him, ugly words, and, I have to admit, some of those stories had the ring of truth. So was I tempted to sell my own version of events? I'd have pocketed a small fortune back then: the girl who travelled the world side by side with Frederick Carruthers – the ringside seat – but I never would have sold a kiss-and-tell. Never considered it for a minute! He was one of my best mates. Naturally, I had my disappointments, nursed them even, on my return. But I kept quiet, I held to my side of the bargain. It's taken me all these years to put pen to paper.

And what a different world it was when we set out in 1970 – more than fifty years ago. Browsing on the internet, I've seen that there are a lot of us out there. The nostalgic boomers who made the journey, publishing memoirs and posting old photos. Some of those old guys converting their slides to modern formats; flashing their memories about. I went overland to India, they declare; I was here, I was there. Hats off to them. None of them could hold a candle to Fred; nothing to compare to our trip.

We had our ups and downs, it goes without saying, and it wasn't all plain sailing, that's for sure; there's always forks in the road. But we were young! And free! We were so lucky, rolling across borders as if we owned the place. That's what bothers me about dear Fred. That he mucked it up so badly: he started out with every advantage, the whole world spread out in front of him. And all that talent. Such a waste.

I don't have children or grandchildren to dedicate this book to. There's no old man in my bed. Will people remember me? My kith and kin, my distant heirs? Will they find a place for me in the family tree? For who remembers an old aunt after she's gone? I'm a believer in correcting the historical record. This is my side of the story. My recollection of these events matters, you understand? I played my own modest part in history. So, do me one thing: promise me that our overland journey won't be forgotten. I've given strict instructions for these papers to be well-preserved. For posterity, a time when I'm no longer around. For future generations. And perhaps, a hundred years from now, some of you not yet born, you'll be handed down some of my valuables – Iznik tiles, maybe, left in a will – and remember this story, and all our misadventures. There are hard, dirty secrets of the heart in these pages, and some honest truths. I'll warn you now, I haven't spared your blushes.

I'm a simple nobody. Plain old Joyce. You won't find me in the newspapers. I'm not sure I'd recognise the girl who set out on that road trip fifty years ago now; Good Lord, to have those pins again, those pretty little tits. No one will tend my flame. I'm not delusional. I am unavailable in print, you won't find my fingerprints in the archives – but I was there, by his side, every single mile. I saw Persia in the time of the Shah, and the sun set over Kabul and the sun rise at the Taj Mahal. I was there too, and this is my story. And your inheritance.

1

London 1970

Kathmandu by van, leave August.
Share petrol and costs.

I didn't always look at the ads at the back of the paper.
Hippies would have called it my karma. A lot of folks on
the road used to talk about karma, as if it got them off the
hook. I've never had much truck with that, as if it could
all boil down to your past lives. Fred used to talk about
karma, as if he didn't have control over his own destiny,
when he had all those advantages and that golden aura.
Handy way of passing on the buck, isn't it? You've got to
make your own reality.

No, it wasn't karma.

I just skimmed down the small ads out of boredom; I
particularly liked the miscellaneous section. Sometimes
people offered up handsome pieces of old furniture,
sometimes they advertised their lonely hearts. These words
jumped out. A few years too late, my first thought; the
Beatles had long been and gone. Everyone knew someone
who'd come back from the hippie trail with dodgy bowels,
claiming wisdom, and eased back into normal society.

I took the train into Clapham from Surbiton. Their gaff was on the southern side of the common, easy to find because its sheer side had been sliced away like white bread by a V2, leaving one beautiful old Georgian house. Chalk white, four storeys high, built for a family. Anton opened the door, his spectacles slipping down his nose, a book propped open in his hand, his fingers carefully placed to hold the page that he'd turned to, as if it was a matter of life and death, and looked at me thoughtfully, like there were hundreds of applicants and I wasn't the only one to inquire, to interrupt his day. He pushed the glasses up his nose.

I thought, at the time, that he owned that grand old house. He presided over the place, and there I was standing on the doorstep. What was I thinking, asking for a ride from this young bloke with a neat little beard? I wasn't fond of boys who spent too much time on their hair. That's just the way I was raised; I expected a man to be a real man. And here I was, asking a favour from this scholar in Oxford brogues, barely out of school. Inside it wasn't so fancy, though; it was makeshift, not quite a squat but uncared for, encrusted pans in the sink and what I now know to be called 'kilims' thrown over Victorian furniture.

You do realise, India is an awfully long way away. We stood there in that front room with all the crap cast about, old tennis shoes on the floor. So, why do you actually want to go? He looked sceptical, as if I wasn't going to cut it. I realised immediately that he wanted something intellectual in answer, so I tried to play ball. I guess I'd like to know more about the Hindis, I said. The Hindus – Hindi is a language, Anton retorted. I didn't think I needed to pass a test, I replied. First impression: arrogant little twit. My face was burning with embarrassment at having been corrected, but he didn't seem to notice. I might not have all your certificates, but I know about real life, I thought. Anton peeved me; I wasn't used to being put straight by a student. No common sense, the sort of brains only good for a game show. He'd be one of those university toffs slamming down the buzzer.

Well, most of the countries we'll go through are Muslim. What about them, and the differences, Shia and Sunni? Did he want a dissertation? I felt like walking away at that point. Do you really want to know why I wanted to go? To get out of the bloody country, to get as far away from Surbiton as possible. But I couldn't say that. It's good to be a little prepared. I have some books you can borrow. But first you need to meet Vera. Come on, I'll take you to see her. Back out through the front door and round to a double-yellowed side road, a Land Rover parked badly across two spaces. Vera meet Joyce, Joyce meet Vera. Why don't you have a decko, check her out, see if she's what you have in mind? It's a long trip, he repeated. He opened the passenger door and left me with the Land Rover as if he'd shown me to a guest bedroom. I walked around the outside first, the paint the exact colour of mould on jam. The back was stacked with military surplus and unappetising boxes, dried food, tins of beans and canned meat. Spare tyre on the bonnet. It was a high step up to the rear door.

Inside it smelled – she, I suppose, smelled – of petrol, old leather and wet Labrador. There was a dirty mackintosh across the back seats, roomy as a garden shed inside and no warmer. A split in the cushion leather where crumbling sponge was pushing through. I could fix that up, I thought, and I knew then that I could be useful to them too. The whole thing needed a clean; no one could be expected to see out of those windows. I climbed over the interior into the front, and the driver's seat was the best place of all. I was barely able to see the windscreen from behind the big black wheel. A solid, vulnerable vehicle, she'd been through a lot already: a warhorse. I liked her a lot more than her owner. You'll look after us, Vera, I thought.

Anton reappeared on the kerbside. There's one more thing. An important thing, essential actually. If you don't mind frightfully you'll have to come back another day, to meet Frederick. Anton looked around as if this Frederick might be there somewhere, under the piles of tarpaulin, though we both knew he wasn't. I clambered down. You have to meet Fred, he said, almost under his breath, as if nothing could proceed without his say-so. I'm afraid he's not here, though, so if you wouldn't mind terribly coming back tomorrow? We could meet at the Queen's Head at lunchtime?

The Queen's Head was a smoky institution on the corner of Clapham Common, the lounge bar's wallpaper flecked with emerald green. A regular talking in a low voice at the bar looked me up and down. I was squinting, after the street, a permanent fug, and somebody was singing a melody, a young boy alone in the back room. Initially, his voice slightly too high, but then he took a low breath and the sound became a long note, cracked at the edges, into profound sorrow, and all the time the thrum of the guitar, and a melody picked along the edges of it. I knew some of those songs, wistful tunes by Joni Mitchell and Carole King.

No sign of Anton or his sidekick. I wondered if they'd decided against me. I was expecting two boys in spectacles. And all the time the singing went on and I waited at the bar for those boys, avoiding eye contact with the old punter. Half an hour, forty-five minutes, and I thought I'd been stood up and went to get my coat when Anton burst in, all earnest apologies, and said, immediately, looking around, but isn't Freddie already here? No, I've been standing here waiting for you both. My irritation might have been showing a little but Anton laughed out loud. Listen – didn't you hear him? And I tuned in again to the guitar strumming from the back room. The song had changed to a harsh repetitive chord, a variation on an old Dylan tune; it was 'Masters of War', if I recall rightly. Those bitter and twisted lyrics – about death planes and bombs, how the masters of war would never be forgiven – in that angelic voice rising high above the twang of notes.

A long-limbed boy, white-blonde, and absolutely absorbed in his own cosmos. Singing for the life of it, and only for himself. Anton said, Fred, you airhead, you were meant to meet Joyce – she's on board! He was sitting on a low-slung sofa, and he stopped playing and stood up – Fred was always a stickler for manners – the guitar dangling from a strap over his arm. He stood taller than I expected from his slender frame, golden flares sitting on his hips. He shook my hand. Cool, Joycie. Pleasure to meet you. Can you drive? Yep. Have you seen our splendid van? Yep. Seen that van and you still want to come? He started playing chords again as if music could just strike up in the middle of a conversation.

When Anton returned with the white wine that I'd asked for, and accepted my warm coins in return, Fred lay back on the sofa near to me, his champagne-coloured hair reflected in the mirror behind him. He offered me a Rothmans. Has Anton been doing his Bamber Gascoigne impression again? I'm sorry, he loves to play quizmaster. They didn't teach Sanskrit at my secondary modern, I said. Just ignore him, you don't need to know anything, just come! Thanks – I was grateful – and we bumped glasses, and I looked into his radiant face. Anyway, why d'you want to come? He had a way of acting as if he'd known you forever, you could tell him anything, all the secrets of the world, all the sex and dark thoughts and dreams of escape, and as if he would listen to them all, and never blink first.

I had been working at the GPO for a few years, and then, that summer, I'd had to take a break, and since then my life hadn't quite got back on track. I'd gone back to plugging: *Who's dialling please? Long-distance? A reverse charge call for you, sir?* Maybe the long-distance calls piqued my curiosity. Now and again I had to interrupt, when it was a pre-paid call, or the line was needed for an emergency. Operator speaking: I am disconnecting this call. Voice neutral, above reproach. And the rushed words, before I snapped them off with a twist of the plug. And the funny thing is they never spoke to me directly, they never said, screw you, operator. They treated me as if I was above them, like I had a godlike power – and I guess I did.

Those foreign city names had made an impression

on me, no doubt about it. My father had recommended Premium Bonds for my savings, and I thought, sod that. And there was decay setting in, the end was nigh. We were being automated, made mechanical, STD – subscriber trunk dialling. The GPO kept celebrating how many countries could be reached, linking up the oceans, dialling directly, without the need for an operator! It was a good time to go.

They nodded; Fred looked satisfied, but it was clear Anton still had doubts about me, sitting prim in his chair with a half, and I wasn't sure we'd rub along so well together. But what choice did I have? To look at, they were like chalk and cheese. Anton was precise, neatly arranged, with a cropped black beard; Fred a sprawling giant next to him, with shoulders honed from rowing 'eights' at his notorious school. I decided then and there that as long as I was with Fred I could put up with his swotty mate.

So the thing you need to know about us is, I love Anton. Antonios Aziz, we love each other don't we, old fruit, Fred said, as if intuiting my doubts about his housemate, and he looped his arm around him tightly. He picked up a couple of darts and started hurling them at the dartboard. An erratic performance, making a hash of it, and laughing as he missed the centre. I will hand it to Fred, he did have *joie de vivre*. Come over here, you uptight bastard, he said, and then Anton was on his feet, playing too. I didn't play much as a kid, Anton said, as a dart bounced off the wall. Apart from with your todger, said Fred and they collapsed into laughter so much that Anton had to hold onto the side of the bar. Later I found out that Fred was the only person who could help Anton relax, to make him goof around. They were a double act, a pairing, sun and moon. When I look back, they were as good as brothers. And on occasion, later, I was jealous, I'll admit, having never had any kind of closeness with Clive. Siblings weren't a joy in my experience. I sensed that, above all, they weren't really that interested in me.

You do know that Anton is the cleverest man you'll ever meet, Fred said to me then, even if he's officially the world's worst darts player. Shut up, Fred, said Anton, bashful and turning pink. He knows so much stuff it would make your brain burst if you knew it all, said Fred, and he really meant it; he admired Anton's talents, and he told me how on prize-giving days there'd be groans from the other boys because Anton would have yet another accolade to collect, for history, for literature, for Latin, shuffling up to the stage to shake the headmaster's hand. Fred sat there clapping loudly and cheering his friend on, bursting with pride. He can do anything he damn well wants. He could be a doctor, a translator for the UN, fancy that! How many young men can say that? He called Anton the Boffin, and Boff, and once some other traveller on the trail thought that was his actual name. Funny how much he liked Anton's conventional achievements, having turned his back on trying to acquire any of his own. I've ruled out college, said Fred, then Anton whispered, I think they've ruled him out, actually. The music was his calling; that was clear.

And why do you want to go on the road, Fred? I returned the question, leaning in as he lit my cigarette. Not much different to you. I want to get away, time for a clean break. He shook out the match. Ever had a heartbreak, Joyce?

But before he could tell me more, Anton returned with a second tray of drinks. Later, I knew that some words had been exchanged at the bar. There had been a murmured consultation, I'll never know what they discussed, did I cut the mustard? Did I have the grit? Would they be taking a risk if they brought a girl along? Was I a bore? Could they survive with me in the Land Rover for months ahead? I didn't look someone who would whinge or make demands, at least, that was my asset. And I had the petrol money, which counted most of all. Fred spoke up for me, I guessed, and he had the upper hand. The requirements were pretty minimal. Come to think of it, I never even knew if there had been any other applicants.

In any case, Anton had been talked round. We both recognised we'd have our work cut out, being cooped up together for months, but alternatives were thin on the ground. I'll stick by Fred's side, I thought, he'll be a hoot. We could leave Thursday week then? They hadn't asked me if I knew anything about exhausts or carburettors or tyre pressures; they had assumed that I wouldn't.

And there were things that I hadn't told them. What was there to tell? No man on the horizon. I had stopped looking. I was just a plain Jane. Plain Joyce. Nothing special. I did all the things that you needed to do: skirt above the knees, hair pulled back, black kohl pulled to the corner of the eyes, and I suppose I did have a kind of grace in my features aged twenty-four. I bloomed for a rose's span, for a journey's length. No spots. A tidy little waist. Even then, I was never going to be the best-looking girl in the room.

The thing is, I'd gone frigid. I didn't like it anymore.

Maybe there would have been a time, but by the time we started the trip, the thought of all that gooey muck and fingering about, like putting your hands in cake dough, well, it made me feel queasy. I didn't want to be touched, and if there was a flickering of interest in my body, unsteady and unreliable, it was like a pilot light ready to go out. I'd even gone off myself. I was no record-breaker, hadn't started until after school, and I suppose there had been a time when there was a thrill. I guess he'd known what to do with himself. Now I was nun-like. And the short hair was part of that. Men had to think twice; I could be mistaken for someone who'd taken a vow, and I was buggered if I was changing for anyone. I had zero intention of putting flowers in my hair.

So we were three. As thrown-together as any people ever could be. But there was one distinguishing mark which we recognised in each other immediately: the desire to flee. Perhaps now, when I consider matters with the wisdom of hindsight, and so many decades later, it was always more of a getting away than a going. We were longing to flee, to fly, to forget.

2

I went home that night, and my parents were sitting waiting up, in front of the television. Two men, a Land Rover, about four months on the road or thereabouts. The destination was Kathmandu, in Nepal – the words felt good on my tongue – and I expected I'd be back round about Christmas, give or take a couple of weeks. There was one hell of a row. My mother clicked the television off and my father stood up as if he might block the door. Isn't it for hippies? my mother said, mouthing the word. What would you want with those kinds of long-haired fellows? They aren't hippies; a lot of kids are doing it nowadays. My father was gentler, shaking his head, the way he had done in recent weeks, in that way that admitted a failure to understand the modern world. After all we've done. And what are we going to tell the neighbours? And we know you've had an upset, love, you don't have to take drastic steps. You can stay in your old room for as long as you like.

Could they actually stop me leaving? My mother tried

all the tricks over the coming days. She'd find me in the kitchen putting the kettle on the stove and say, it's not for people like us. It's risky for a woman on her own, which, admittedly, years later, I did agree with. She swung between pleading and accusing barbs. And the clincher, at every opportunity: who are these peculiar fellows in any case? You don't know anything about them. Their determination to keep me in Surbiton made me even more determined to be anywhere else. And, I'll admit, their incomprehension, especially of Clive and his wife, gave me a little puff of inflation. I could already feel the lure of turning my back. The feeling was there alright, every time I looked around my family at the dinner table.

The things that had been planned out for me were gravy and suet and custard. Alright if you fancied them, bloody horrible if you weren't in the mood. Secretarial college, a part-time job to follow, children without a doubt. A lot of semi-detached houses in our suburbs. Nice long gardens, my mother said. How to break out of them? What to do once you'd smashed the windows? As school had trailed off, I was turning up, going home, doing the bare minimum, allowing my real mind to live outside the classroom, floating in music magazines and records and the belief that David Bowie might descend one day in a puff of smoke and save me.

My father dawdled one morning before work. Took me for a walk with the dog. Look, your mother's getting her knickers in a twist. I understand you wanting to see the world, wouldn't have minded seeing a bit of it myself, but all this talk of a van, it seems a little extreme. If you wanted to go somewhere, France, say, and spend some time learning French, that we could go along with. The world is a big place. You've got your whole life ahead of you. It had been holidays in a borrowed caravan for us. My father had been places in the war, but those names – Tripoli, Libya, Tobruk – seemed as dusty and vacant to me as the pews of the parish church. It didn't count as travel in our book if you'd been sent off there in khaki. Later I learned that Fred's father, Lord Charles Carruthers, was a real war hero, with proper gongs. Ribbons and swords, the works. There's even a painting, quite a decent mid-twentieth-century oil – you might have seen it? – hanging in the National Portrait Gallery.

I had the copies of books which Anton had insisted I borrow – he'd inscribed his name on the inside page – about Buddhism and Hinduism. I ignored them for a few days, had a flick through, couldn't get a handle on that whole cosmic order made up of so many gods. Where the hell did I imagine I was going? The closest I'd ever been to India was a school trip to the Commonwealth Institute in South Ken, life-sized models of peasants with their skirts hitched up, ankle-deep in pretend water, picking paddy. I'd handled a small elephant in the gift shop, encrusted in tiny mirrors – oh my word, how I'd wanted that elephant! – it was much too expensive. I stood next to a rack of postcards and glanced at the cashier who was busy with customers. I found myself slipping that elephant into my pocket without paying. I'm ashamed to admit it now, but I was only a kid, I couldn't help myself. I just had to own that object.

And then there was the corner shop at the end of our road, like every other road in England by that time. My mother warned me not to linger in there. She didn't like the smell. To be honest, she probably had some prejudices about foreigners. She did come out with some daft things about Asians. I used to think she was too hung up, although as I've got older, I've come round to realising I shouldn't have judged her so harshly.

But despite all the arguments, I never thought about staying; the thought never even crossed my mind. In the end they came round to it, threw a little leaving party the night before, just the three of us, with Babycham in the best glasses and KP nuts in the nibble bowls. Even my mother had another drink, and held my left hand aloft and placed a gold band on the fourth finger, like a bride – she'd heard it was safer that way – and then she looked at me with pity because we could both see the mark where the skin was distinctly paler, where a ring had once sat; she kissed me on my cheek.

Tom used to say the best thing about the sixties was the pill. He used to nag me about it as he fondled me through my shirt, putting his hands over my breasts, as if they were headlamps, two at a time. Go and see the GP, he'll put you straight. I wrote a letter to an agony aunt, *Should you go on the pill because your boyfriend (correction, fiancée) is pleading with you to do it?* They never printed it – the editor must have thought, well, it's better than the alternative for a young girl; that was the attitude in those days. There were still ghosts around, backstreet butchers, and mother-and-baby homes.

I hadn't been fully formed. My likes and dislikes came and went like monthly adverts in *Jackie* magazine; groups on *Top of the Pops*, television stars with perms, a small glass snow-shaker which showered down confetti on a happy couple. Even my possessions were a kid's, and the wedding gifts, when they came, were meant to catapult me into another world. Cutlery sets laid out in tiny suitcases with velvet lining and brass buckles; that's what people thought transformed you into an adult. And people said the most ridiculous things: you're becoming a woman now, a woman of the world, as if that could be achieved by acquiring a Denby gravy boat. So maybe it wasn't all Tom's fault; I hated every trapping.

He was Clive's mate. Would have been alright with a few pounds off the middle, a decent haircut, less of a temper. I thought I could fix him up once I had him all to myself. He was a decorator, had wallpaper swatches in his pockets, offered an 'interior decorating service', as he described it, and I hear he's done well for himself, over the years, he believed – rightly, as it happens – that people would spend a hell of a lot of cash on making their houses to die for in the future. Wooed me with his multicolour patter, his rainbow sales pitch. He told me we'd decorate our house with coordinated colours. When I closed my eyes it had seemed like a soft landing, all those plump cushions. More fool me.

I realise this is a detour from the journey, but it's all part of the story. I'm trying to help you understand why I had to leave. Would I have gone if I'd known how it would all turn out? I swear I wouldn't have changed a bloody thing. I had made my getaway.

A week on Thursday, as arranged, Clive dropped me to the house before his first job. I think he wanted to sniff them out, and get a good look at them. Anton and

Freddie, what names. Names that said a lot even before I knew them. Couple of knobs, Clive muttered; are you sure they know how to drive? Outside the house, Anton was looking worried, peering in the bonnet, checking the oil with a dipstick, and Fred was nowhere to be seen. Clive refrained from getting involved with the engine. Then Fred flounced down the steps, out into the road, in his charming way, channelling all those ancestors, military commanders and naval captains, with epaulettes and derring-do. He clasped Clive by the hand – profuse thanks, old boy – and sent him packing.

Clive left me behind in that late-August drizzle; the smell of tarmac rising from the London streets and a faint whiff of rubbish from the metal bins. So you're on board, said Anton, as if he'd wagered that I wouldn't come. Of course she is; Joyce is a good egg, aren't you? Freddie said and he reached out his arms wide to embrace me like an old friend, and I clocked then that he was wearing an Afghan coat, ginger orange, puffed up around his collar like a lion's mane, and thought of what Clive would be reporting back to Surbiton.

Departing at twelve noon; the ferry sailing at five o'clock. Time for a celebratory spliff, Fred said, and he rolled up on the bonnet. I took a drag as if it was something I was used to. The smoke was overpowering and I stifled the cough in my throat.

Every part of the rear was jammed, metal boxes strapped to the roof. We have gallon jerry cans, some for water and some for petrol (don't bloody well mix them up, Anton said). Sleeping bags, paraffin, a tarpaulin which can be fixed to the side of the van to make a shelter if anyone can ever put the damn thing up, a Trangia, mess tins, enamel mugs. Some of this is old army gear, I found it all in a barn at Fred's place. Will you be alright in the back there, Joyce?

At exactly twelve noon Anton banged the roof. He was proud of the radio, which had been wired up to run off the battery. Inside the van, Anton driving, Freddie in the passenger with his feet raised up against the dashboard, the window wound down fully, despite the cold crosswind, and I knew that they were nervous to get going, and scratching their heads as they always would be for every day of every week ahead about Vera: would she let us down? I took up my place in the rear seats and studied them for the first time from behind, as I would do many times in the weeks to come.

Fred's Roman profile, looking out of the window, strands of blonde hair hanging on either side of his parting. He brushed it out of his eyes continually, his fidgeting, restless, skinny body shifting again and again in the passenger seat. Occasionally he'd turn round to offer me a wink or a puff. And Anton, firm brown hands on the wheel, checking the mirror, the grimace of earnest concern on his face, readjusting his glasses. We were set, we were settling in.

And I was there, fully present. Vera gave us every bump, I felt every undulation, and I gripped the seat in front and gave an inner whoop of joy. We crawled through Peckham, Lewisham, Sidcup, stopping at lights, letting the ladies with their little dogs and hats go over the zebras. Vera was a growler, a slow beast, a slow burner. I trusted her with my life. A steady 50 mph was what Anton had based his calculations on. I had never felt so sure that something was really going to happen in my life. The lights changed to green as we entered Dover.

3

We stood on the deck and I looked back at the white cliffs in all their spitfire glory, and I felt nothing but elation.

Time for an aperitif, Fred said – I'm not sure I knew what one was at that point – but then he led us along galleries and staircases down to the ferry bar (he was good at locating bars) and ordered three Pernod and one for the bargirl too – a petite little thing, leaning over and leaving precious little to the imagination – with a wink. This was the first time I'd seen Fred in action, and he was a master of his craft.

Fred and Anton up high on stools at the bar; I was at an angle to them, as if I might have been a stranger. And Anton shifted his back to me, as they talked, turning to Fred like a plant to the sun. They were straight out of the same stable, despite their differences. I figured out they'd been to the same school, shared a dormitory, and then after sixth form Anton had stayed with Freddie at the Clapham house, which was a kind of family heirloom used by his father when he wanted to see his accountant or visit his club, something he did less and less. The house had been taken over by a wide network of cousins and siblings who used it for shagging or hanging out in the capital, passed in and out, multiple keys mushrooming across southern England.

That afternoon the boys reminisced about old pranks and scrapes, a different vocabulary of fourth-formers and boiler rooms and playing fields and sanitoria. There was nothing for me to add at all to their chat about this or that prefect. Perhaps I was a little sullen, as I watched the barmaid and understood for the first time how much went before. I wanted to be as central to their lives as they were to mine, you see, or as they were to each other, our funny little triangle to replace their double act. And then Fred swivelled round to me, realising I was still there, and squeezed my arm. Are we talking shop again? Naughty boy, Anton, say sorry to Joyce.

I'd never known men like them; I knew chippies, brickies, sparkies, who had done a few years on a building site or some other trade by their age. They bought rounds and drank with their old men, and had often already married; they even had sprogs, like my brother Clive, who had a wife who wore stockings and a hat, and owned a lawnmower. They weren't fiddling about, wondering about life. They were up and at it. So these twenty-year-olds with their own little daydreams and self-absorbed melodies, well, I couldn't quite take them seriously. I had every reason to doubt their ability to keep the vehicle going; I was stuck with them, and they with me. I didn't know if I could fit in.

The second night we stayed in a youth hostel in Austria

by a lake – I forget exactly where – and ordered sausages, which came floating in a pan of water with bottles of dark beer. There was still a formality in passing the salt, in watching each other and knowing we were bound together in a world of strangers. It had been a couple of days of monotonous driving and we spoke little, our eyes ringing with the noise of the engine, arse-sore from sitting. The place was a postcard, with Alpine mountains all around. The air had a freshness, like sucking on a peppermint, and I took a walk with Fred. I guess I was still wary of Anton and his sharp tongue, fearful of saying something plain stupid in front of him. Even thanking waiters, *merci, danke schön*, was a concentrated effort; I felt he'd judge my lousy pronunciation, and so I stuck close to Fred's side during those early days.

Fred said to me, look, don't mind Anton, he's a brick. He's never let me down. And, well, actually, things are a bit different for him. He meant he didn't have the same sort of dosh, that was already clear to me. Anton's going to have to knuckle down before long. His mother thinks he's going to be a doctor like his old man. But between you and me, he's made an application to the School of Oriental and African Studies, he's getting up the guts to tell her he wants to be a linguist. He'd rather die than be a doctor. He doesn't want to handle the bodies of strange people. He's having a bash at Farsi. I'd already noticed the books as big as breeze blocks, completely impractical for the trip, taking up pride of place in the back of the Land Rover. That's when I started to understand how different the two of them were; Fred didn't have to worry his pretty head about making a living. Fred stubbed out his cigarette on the dirt track and we went back to the farmhouse, ready to drive again.

They bickered a little about the route to Turkey. Fred thought we should just race through and, though I didn't dare say, I agreed with him. We sped through chunks of Europe, I realise now, avoiding the cost. Never set eyes on the Eiffel Tower or the Colosseum. Dummies. Pissing in horrible French holes, learning not to squat with anything in your pocket. I must have had my first period of the trip around then – I'll spare you the gory details, except to say it's not something you hear about much in those memoirs by blokes on the overland; that's a bit they leave out. Managing all that, with no toilet paper and a bucket; I got used to it. Women always find solutions.

Anyway, the route wasn't mine to choose, nobody had asked me to drive yet, no one had asked my advice. They were taking it in turns. Fred's driving was cavalier; he liked to keep one hand on his thigh and then lunge for the gear stick at the last minute. Vera didn't like to be pushed, but Fred wasn't the type to slow down.

We spent a night in Bari before we caught the ferry to Corfu; Anton got his own way, he insisted on seeing the duomo, the castles and the little piazzas. Then Fred refused to get up that morning. I wasn't too thrilled to be left sightseeing with Anton by myself, truth be told. I was sure he was still assessing me, and that he might start quizzing me on all the things I didn't know about the world. But to my surprise he just started talking, and quite openly too. He said that when he looked at a wall, or a painting, he saw layers of time, and heard all the voices clamouring from way back to speak about what they'd been through.

He was good on dates and wars and maritime victories. Clive would have thought it was showing off, but despite myself I was hooked.

We walked in silence for a while along the jetty, watching sailing boats play on the water, and I had a feeling Anton wanted to broach something. Maybe it was money? Or the driving? I was still on the lookout for offences I could have committed. Joyce, listen, he had stopped by the sea-wall, I wanted to have a word with you. I'm worried – maybe that's too strong – I'm concerned, about Fred, will you keep an eye on him for me? He's... temperamental. He corrected himself – he's special. We continued walking back towards the complicated backstreets woven tightly behind the harbour. I thought if the two of us watch out for him, you see, that would help, Fred can be... erratic. He doesn't always know when to stop. He doesn't always look after himself.

I have to admit I was rather cheered up by this turn of events. And I had my first inkling then that I might know what was best for Fred. I could keep an eye on him, of course, I'd be delighted to!

I discovered that Fred's heartbreak was part of their reason for heading east. The girl in question was older than Freddie; she'd been studying something grand at Cambridge, a subject which I'd never heard of, anthropology. Gloucestershire too, probably related if you went far back along the family tree, Anton said. Freddie had been smitten. He'd been driving up from London in one of the brassy motors that his dad owned, wooing her with country picnics and carving their initials on a tree.

The earl egged him on, Anton went on, said she was a

good bit of stuff. Marriage material. You know, they want you to get with the right sort of girl, Anton said, kind of sadly. And then Fred had some kind of... nervous collapse.

So I'd been thinking about the trip for a while, he said, and we got hold of Vera, and I was saying, come on Fred, how about it, a change is as good as etcetera, and that's when he started playing a few more tunes, and looking at maps occasionally, although I still don't think he's got the faintest idea where we're actually going.

All of it was beyond my experience; I'd never been in a convertible, I'd never met anyone who'd been to Cambridge. I was starting to realise I wanted to be part of it all, that this was the start of a connection that could last a lifetime. Looking back, and not wanting to exaggerate my importance, I knew then that I was the ideal passenger. I was just the person they needed to help them on this trip, even if they didn't realise it themselves yet. I could be useful, and keep an eye on them, and bring them both back home safely. Meanwhile that girl – she was called Felicity – with her airs and graces and her abilities to open champagne properly, she had it all, including the ability to break Fred's heart. What happened to Felicity? I asked. Anton said she went off travelling with some Frenchman, heir to a textile fortune. We'd reached a square with a drinking fountain, close to the *pensione*. Come on, he looped his arm through mine, let's find our lead singer, it's time to get back on the road.

On the ferry out of Bari – towards Corfu, across the Ionian sea – we could forget the car for a night and a day, leave her in the hull of the ferry, her wheels stopped with wooden wedges to prevent her sliding backwards.

We had a cabin, four bunks for the three of us, with a little washbasin in one corner, and Fred pulled down the beds so we could sit up on high, dangling our legs over the edge. The porthole was blurry – we were on the waterline – and we looked out as if there was a view. Anton was out on the deck. Fred was rolling a cigarette, sitting on the lower bunk. The motion of the boat was gentle, lurking, ever-present. Ever had your heart broken, Joycie? he said to me, and I wasn't sure what to say. Had I? I thought I had, at that time.

Her name was Felicity, he said, unlucky for some. I pretended to be surprised and he told me, in a matter-of-fact way, how he brought her off pretty quickly, with his fingers, and she admitted to him that no one had done it that way before, and he wasn't sure about it when she let out noises which were a bit frightening, they could have been noises of pain or fury. She seemed so relaxed afterwards. He thought that was what he could give her. He didn't know that she wanted something else. That was just a bonus and, he found out, not what she really wanted. What happened, in the end? She went off travelling with some Frenchman. Oh God, just talking about this makes me horny, Joyce. I didn't know what to say, I'd never met anyone so prepared to talk about sex as Fred, as if he was talking about the weather.

Fred started looking for company on that ferry in earnest and that evening he appeared in a dinner jacket with a bottle of white wine under his arm. Captain's table, mates. Where on earth did you get that from? Anton said, looking at his white jacket, blonde hair slicked back. Freddie was abandoning us to the canteen and heading for the silver-service restaurant. I wanted to hear that chick play piano. Her name's Sophia, she's from Yugoslavia, she's got a complicated relationship with the Greeks. Getting into a complicated relationship with the English, Anton retorted. Going to take a peek into the dining room. You two don't mind, do you? I'll see you later. We didn't see Freddie again that night and he didn't return to our cabin and Anton didn't mention it when we woke up so neither did I.

4

The next morning, after breakfast, I stood on the deck with Anton, the blue stretching out on either side. The coastline of Corfu or a line of cloud on the horizon.

Anton didn't suit the sea, he was an urban person. He looked awkward in the breeze, with his arms steadying him on the railings. Are you seasick? I asked. There was barely a ripple on the water. Just cold, he sniffed. Take this, I said, and handed him my cardy, which had been my dad's and was several sizes too big for me, moth-eaten. He pulled it on over his head in one swift action.

I was, I'll admit, curious about Fred's family, to say the least. He dropped hints now and then about the house and I realised he was from an important family, naturally, but I hadn't quite been able to piece the Carruthers puzzle together. So I took my chance that morning to ask Anton about Fred's father.

Well, his old man is charming, of his generation, Anton said. The park has become his life's work now. Determined not to give it up to the National Trust. Complains that the others don't fight hard enough, just hand their houses over the minute they hit rocky times. He's my benefactor. I shouldn't say a word against him. Benefactor? Well, it's no state secret, he paid my school fees for the last two years of boarding, to my mother's great shame and relief, and he's helping me out with university, buying books, the room in Clapham...

What a different world they inhabited, with their parks and benefactions and constant string of names that I couldn't locate. You know he's an earl, right? This was a shock. I thought it was just a nickname for Lord Carruthers. And he's drop-dead gorgeous, naturally. A hit with the ladies. That part wasn't surprising to me; Fred must have got it from somewhere. It wasn't always an easy thing for Fred, his dashing old man. I think that's been a source of friction. He grinned, and he looked very good at that moment himself, in my father's old jumper, with his hair all sticking up from the breeze, and the black glimmer of stubble on his cheeks. Anton added that the earl had been the governor of a small colony which had slipped out of British hands in 1960. Not an important place relative to other countries, a speck along a coastline, one where, Anton said, they gave us a run for our money. I personally knew bugger all about that kind of history. Guv'nor. Governess. Government. Could have been a policeman for all I cared in those days. I can tell you, though, I've learned a hell of a lot more about it since then.

Freddie came from what Anton described as an old pile. Pile of shit was how Freddie described it, shrugging as if it was a nasty memory that he didn't want to go into. I didn't hold back my questions after that – perhaps you'll think I was a nosey parker – and so I learned, mainly from Anton when Freddie wasn't there, all about its Doric columns and massive symmetrical windows. Palladian, he called it, savouring the word. Anton's eyes glittered with the love of it. He'd stayed there for a couple of summers during the school holidays, sleeping in a four-poster, and the boys had sculled about in an old boat on the stream. Anton told me everything, willingly, over the weeks: how the house had been built from Bath stone the colour of uncooked pastry. Some cottages swiped out of the way two hundred years ago so that the original Carruthers could get a better view, a dead straight view down to the lake and the fountain at the end of the long walk. Sheep dotted on the surrounding fields – they owned everything as far as the eye could see – and then acres of woodland. Proper lord of the manor.

All wasn't well, though. Ice on the inside of the windows, mouse droppings, frescoes peeling, strategically placed buckets, chunks of ceiling just missing the heads of visitors. Freddie's old man on some sort of cycle of endless, hopeless restoration – Anton compared it to a classical punishment. Several rooms under dust sheets. And he'd like Fred to lend a hand, but Fred is no help at all. He's alright, the earl is better than Fred makes out. You've probably heard Fred complaining about him. He finds him a little, well, abhorrent. He was good to me, gave me a lovely little Persian manuscript from the library as a gift before we left. He thinks I'm a positive influence on Fred, his swotty friend. Anyway, we're all furious with our parents, aren't we? Anton had a point. Maybe Freddie just showed it all on the outside, like his clothes and his music, everything dangling out there for people to steal, whereas my anger was a hard little bottled thing.

Then Anton corrected himself. He's the heir, his father wants him to run the place, step up to the job. He bangs on a lot about duty. And then there was his mother, all that. Lord Carruthers wasn't the right person to help Freddie along when his mother got her diagnosis. That went without saying. Young Fred, alone in all those cold rooms, and long halls, without someone to look out for him. He had sisters but Fred was the first-born son. It put him under pressure. Poor old Fred, I said, and we both smiled, pitying our rich friend, and feeling better about what we'd been handed in life.

The following afternoon in Corfu, I had the feeling that we should stop there and stay forever. There was no need to head eastward. What more could anyone ever need than this turquoise sea, these balconies on cobbled streets? I'd come from Surbiton, remember. I also had – when I looked at the strange land stretching away for so many miles and thought of continuing the journey – an ominous feeling. I was unnerved. Was it a bellyache? I had spoken to a shopkeeper that day – I was buying a penknife for myself from a stall selling strange hunting weaponry and the man had given me a stern warning, unasked for. Those countries further east, they have bad people. Cruel people, he repeated, running the blade along his finger. Is it an exaggeration to say I felt dread? Why bother, I said to the boys that afternoon, nothing can beat this place. They wouldn't contemplate it. They had made up their minds. Naturally it was Fred who scotched any of my plans to stay in Greece. He was determined then, the most desperate to get to India, especially once we went down to Kontogialos beach that evening.

Fred had got wind of a rumour that some travellers had arrived down there, heading in the other direction, back from India. The beach was a long crescent, and we saw them immediately at the other end, under the glow of the full moon, their VW parked where the esplanade met the sand. Fred announced we were heading to Kathmandu, and they stumbled up the beach towards us, greeted us like lost friends. You've got to go, they urged, as if there were wonders in store for us we couldn't ever imagine. You've got to go. English accents, some German and Italian too; they all spoke with an international lilt, they'd been on the road for weeks, possibly months, none of them was very good on the details. Come and smoke, they said, and they sat in a circle on the sand with their spliffs. A man, lean and beautiful in a kaftan, was playing a bamboo flute, turning and spinning, his pregnant lover sat watching with her legs crossed.

Their clothes were costumes: feathers in headbands, garlanded with beads and flowers, performing for each other, making a spectacle of themselves. I'd never seen anything like that show. Their colourful smocks and wide trousers with crazy rivets and buckles, strange tattoos on ankles and shoulder blades. And you should have seen the way one of them was dancing, reaching up to the moon, yacking on about a whole new way of life. They hardly had anything: hammocks and candles and blankets. They called themselves flower children.

We ended up camping with them for the night. In the morning, the clothes were gone, they were naked, swimming in the sea, the women walking easily around, showing off the dark hair under their arms, between their legs. Anton raised his eyebrows, said quietly to me, I've had enough of this, let's go.

They're alright, I said. They aren't harming anyone. Because I realised then, seeing how they lived, that there was something in it, that some of their ideas might work. I wouldn't want you to think I was against hippies back then, nothing like that. I'd seen them around in London, certainly, but I'd never spoken to any before. I looked at the girl in a trailing muslin dress with a sparkly Indian mark in the middle of her forehead. The night before she'd told me how she'd started out from Haight-Ashbury. What an easy way of being in the world, I thought, maybe she does have an answer. All these young people dancing together, spinning away from an old centre, revelling in themselves. They talked about making love, the end of wars, and the women had a look about them like they were constantly at it, and the men walked around proudly, cock of the walk, because they were getting so much. I can admit to envy. They didn't like governments and they didn't want to work, and they'd found a way to do whatever the hell they liked.

As I say, it wasn't that I was against hippies per se. There was merit in some of their ideas, granted, though I would be embarrassed to be seen out with those characters in the street today, with their tie-dyed waistcoats over hairy chests – wouldn't want to walk down Clapham High Street with them, would you? My niece says the current term is soap-dodgers. And some of them, to tell the truth, weren't that, well, fragrant. And they took every chance they could to scrounge off the state – it was easy in those days to fiddle the dole, and plenty of them managed to claim it while on the road by sending an impersonator down the social.

That afternoon the beach was the perfect temperature. Early September warmth. Fred didn't want to leave. He swam elegantly, going out too far into the bay, and I was trying not to look at his lithe back, the slightly crooked spine; his arse covered in pale fuzz. In the end we persuaded him to climb back in the van and drive away from the crowd, the lurid VW visible for a long time in the distance. We drove back towards the town and its little lanes with white bedsheets hung to dry across every street, and it was our last afternoon in Corfu. Suddenly, having met those freaks, the prospect of getting to India was real, right in front of us, if we just stayed on that road and kept our heads. And there was a rising sense of adventure in the van, and I agreed then, I wanted to press on and leave Europe behind.

People call it the hippie trail now. As if it was one thing, and we were moving in one long caravan. It wasn't anything like that, and the important thing to remember is that we weren't all freaks. In fact, me, Anton, Freddie – the three of us – were definitely overlanders, and there was a clear partition line between us and the other tribe. We were in a Land Rover for starters; that set us apart, especially a Landy with a spare seat. Freaks didn't have the cash for that. Hippies took their time, their number-one priority was to smoke, and they'd often been on the road a lot longer, backwards and forwards between India and Istanbul. They'd soak up bits and pieces about the countries they were travelling through, like sea sponges, but never applied themselves to learning. Anton was especially keen to make sure we were distinguished from that lot.

I use the word 'freaks' not to put them down, but because that's what they called themselves. Nobody called themselves a 'hippie'. We are the counterculturalists, my dear, Fred liked to declare. Americans were Beatniks. Anton preferred 'Bohemians'. Some people said 'longhairs', which sounds quite strange today. Was I any of these things? Where did I fit in? I didn't have long hair – mine was cut close, all cropped and boyish. And I wasn't a pothead: I didn't care much for the substances.

Fred scored some grass from that crowd in Corfu but he said it was weak, it made a glorified cigarette. He usually had one on the go or rolled behind his ear after that. Anton didn't like us smoking in the van but Fred ignored him, kept the windows rolled down. We were all on a little bit of something in those days, just to take the edge off life – and you mustn't think any less of me if I admit to the odd puff in this story too. But I never let myself get out of control. I always had my wits about me. And I haven't touched the stuff for decades – nowadays I prefer a couple of glasses of a fine red. I find a quality decanter improves the experience. In fact, I've developed quite the taste for Cabernet Sauvignon.

They let me drive for the first time somewhere east of Corfu. Fred scrambled out of the driver's seat and I took control of Vera and drove her fast and straight over the potholes and along the switchbacks on the road up to Katerini. Easy tiger, he said. That was rich coming from him. I felt that something had changed, though, by driving them both, that there was a resetting of an equilibrium, that I hadn't complained or asked for advice, and I kept a steady pace and an even hand, and managed the road in the allotted time, without a scrape or an incident, blasting the horn at the livestock in the road when necessary and changing the radio with one hand, to that recent Stones song that Fred liked so much, and which was completely at odds with the setting, the shoddy little villages with tin roofs and goat pens and olive trees. I didn't tell them that I was far too low behind the wheel, made a mental note to use a pillow next time, to add a few inches, to raise myself up so I could see the full road. The boys mucked about to 'Sympathy for the Devil' in the back – Anton manically pretending to drum on the armrest with his fingers, Fred miming air guitar, both wailing at the top of their voices. Woo – woo-woo. They begged me to turn the track up, so the whole van rattled with the bass. They sang that Rolling Stones song again and again, woo-ing out the window together all the way to Turkey.

I had a vision there, as I drove, of what my future might look like and knew, whatever happened, that this was a crucial junction point in my life. That the tracks, like on Clive's old train set, were at a turntable, and I was going to take off in a new direction. Or, as my mother might have said, that there was more than one way to skin a cat. And I understood for the first time that I could run away from Surbiton but still have an English life. That I didn't have to leave everything behind forever. That I would return home, go back and sort myself out; a better, improved, more independent version, just as it has worked out in fact. My own home, some beautiful possessions. Just like the place I sit here to write. I didn't know yet how I was going to achieve that, but I knew I was going back to better things. That I was going to make my own fate.

I'm a pretty straightforward person, no-nonsense, as my nieces describe me. I don't like dwelling on the past or the future too much, staying in the present is what I've always tried to do, so writing down my memories of the overland trip now is quite a disconcerting experience, I'll admit, thinking back to those days when life was so different for young people. We had carte blanche. The possibility to start again. To rewrite our story. No nasty tales could follow us along the road, there was no 'social media'. And afterwards, when things turned out... somewhat imperfectly, let's say, the slate could be wiped clean too. Never any need to relive those old experiences, no indulging ourselves by wallowing in old pictures or mawkish sentiment about tragic loss. And we were far better off for it, wouldn't you agree? No mobile phones or emails, of course; when we departed, we were saying goodbye for good, and the best we might expect was an occasional letter from home.

The only way to keep in touch was through letters, which we'd pick up from poste restante along the way, though I could have done without my post in Thessaloniki: a letter from Clive, typical one-sided thing, that managed to make me feel both guilty for leaving and glad to be away in one go.

Fred had something much grander. Pages and pages of airmail paper, brittle and blue. My father likes the sound of his own voice, he said, and he flipped the pages so quickly I was certain he couldn't have been reading what was written. Even dull letters were exciting in my world. And then Fred just scrunched it all up into a ball, without hesitation, in his fist, and chucked it into the bin.

You can't do that. Why not? It's taken us bloody ages to find this post office. I was tempted to fish the thing out, though the bin was dirty and covered in bird droppings. Same old *pater familias*. Same old news. Just because he deigned to write it down? Well, he bothered to write, I said, thinking of my own family, and the way that letters were venerated and placed on the mantelpiece. It's transient, Fred said, just thoughts. What did it say? That he hopes I don't waste all my time on the guitar and make sure I see the Parthenon, although I've told him several times that we are not going to Athens. And there's a whole lot of stucco they've discovered on the west wing of the house, which he's dying to show Anton, and Anton will be just longing to see that when we get back, won't he just. When I leaned over the bin, as we left, I could decipher the scrawl: Your loving father. I don't need to read every word of his poppycock, Fred said, watching me peer into the dustbin. Why do you hate him so much? I asked. Huh, he looked at me uncertainly, as if I'd said something inappropriate. I never said that. Did I say that?

PART 2

THE PUDDING SHOP

5

Near the Turkish border, heading towards Istanbul, another hippie vehicle – a large, tatty Bedford bus, once painted orange, covered in coloured slogans and symbols – had broken down by the side of the road. Skinny guys lay on the roof and sat on the verge, and Anton said, ignore the freaks, can't get their mechanical shit together, can they? Drive on. A man in a turban stood under the bonnet, straining to twist a part with a spanner. Fred, with a childish pout, braked and parked up and offered them a hand, asked if they needed water for the radiator or enough diesel to get them to the next town. They said not to worry, we should drive on, they'd see us again at the Pudding Shop. Afterwards, as we pulled away, Fred said, Anton, don't be so fucking judgemental.

From that moment on, the Pudding Shop became a bit of an obsession for Fred, he was so focused on getting there. The three words became a kind of mantra, a stand-in for Istanbul itself. What's all the fuss about the Pudding

Shop? Anton asked when we were approaching Istanbul. You'll see, said Fred.

The Pudding Shop was the first name on the trail, a convening point, a sort of accidental hub. God alone knows how the owners had managed to make their place an essential lodestar for thousands of westerners, it was a shabby little haunt. There were other unlikely stops like that, places that had sprung up like lightbulbs on a wire, wayfarer points, where you had to stop to get the news and the gossip, or just to meet someone who spoke English or who could help you with whatever you needed help with: petrol, an international dialling code, sanitary towels, a lift, we all needed something. And those names became incantations, punctuation points – Chicken Street, Freak Street – and around those places the traders multiplied, bringing in everything that we wanted, Cadbury's chocolate bars and cold Cokes, so even if we were pinching our pennies, every now and then you got a little touch of luxury, a little reconnection with home.

In Istanbul the markets sold all the things travellers liked to wear; then out came the harem pants, better to pull down your trousers quicker to squat on a roadside. The guys liked waistcoats with endless pockets to store matches and notebooks and phone numbers and hostel addresses on scraps of paper. People needed things that could wash and dry quickly in the sun. There was a sort of logic to the fashion that people wouldn't understand nowadays. I resisted it, stuck to my jeans and T-shirt, determined not to be mistaken for a freak. Fred was into baggy pants before we got to Turkey.

I am sure there were minarets on the horizon and

twinkling lights on the Bosporus as we rolled in, though all I remember now is the focus on the Pudding Shop. We found it easily, saw the big signboard in red capitals: Lale Café. While Anton was parking up, I went inside with Fred, pushing open the wooden door and sitting down quickly at a table, sensing the gaze of the travellers sizing us up, nakedly inexperienced. A waiter welcomed new arrivals paternally, watching them like children left to roam in a restaurant, choosing what they wanted from the menu without the disapproval of parents.

A humble café with mirrored walls on one side, panelling on the other, rows of wooden tabletops and benches crammed to the rafters. It was easy to distinguish between those who were travelling east and those who were travelling west. At every table freaks on their way back into Europe, or the new seekers on their way out. The ones returning thinner, more chiselled, with a swagger of experience, their bodies marked with the journey. The skin of those returnees was saturated with smoke and tattoos and with a kind of smirk of wisdom which Fred longed for. You see, Fred hankered to be taken seriously by the older guys who'd already done the trip. They sat at bigger tables in cliques and looked at ease with each other. And the new starters, like us, a couple hunched over a road map and a cluster from a bus in clean denim, skin like buttered mash, looking apprehensively at the menu. Freddie wandered casually over to the counter, inspecting the dishes as if he was used to eating Turkish pudding at all hours of the day and night, then sauntered back.

A man with his back to us leaned on the rear legs of his chair so that his head was close to the edge of our table.

He wore a horrid little bolt of silver in his nose, above his brown moustache. You kids got your visas? Got to watch it near Dogubayazit, there's a whole lot of shit going down, man. Some very uptight policemen these days. I've done this trip four times now and never seen it so bad. They will bang you up for grams, believe me. Be careful, kiddos, don't do anything I wouldn't do. The guy came from Glasgow and had gone as far as Bangkok. His friend had fair hair matted into dreadlocks, wore a red bandana and said nothing at all.

The man said he went back and forth, across continents, and didn't explain how he afforded to, or why he did it. He talked about how it used to be a few years ago, with Afghan border guards who'd have a smoke with you and wave you through, and hand you woollen blankets or a pakul (which I figured out was some kind of hat) as gifts, and gave us the feeling that we had come too late, that the good times had already ended. I looked at the mirrored walls, and the big pans of warm, unfamiliar food. Freddie kept the conversation going, accepting his suggestions and warnings.

The orange Bedford we'd passed on the road pulled up outside and the passengers came tumbling into the Pudding Shop; Fred scooted along the bench to make room for them, his eyes glistening at the prospect of all these new people. Their bus was covered in stickers and graffiti and had set out from London about a week before us. The bus had trundled its way over the Alps which, by all accounts, wasn't guaranteed to happen, and there were a lot of stories about the failings of that vehicle which everyone always called 'the Magic Bus' with a touch of irony.

I liked the driver, a Punjabi lad called Harjit, a kid from Birmingham whose dad worked shifts in a steel mill. Harjit had been to one of the grammars and spoke English absolutely perfectly, unless you counted the Birmingham accent and, by God, he liked a spliff – he could cane them one after the other. My mum thinks I'm going to meet some aunties to get a bride, he said, and that's why they let me drive this rust bucket to India. He had no intention of bringing anything back apart from the finest hashish. He said his mum and dad were stuck in the past, and his sister was snogging a Pakistani guy, and she was going to have the Battle of Britain on her hands if they ever found out about him. Harjit had borrowed or hired the Magic Bus, it wasn't clear how, and sold the seats for sixty quid a pop, and now he was worried as hell that the banger wouldn't make it past Turkey, as were all his passengers.

And there were a couple of weirdos on that Magic Bus, granted – like Tattoo Face, a girl who sat sullen and moody as a monsoon cloud, and barely spoke to anyone. Don't think I ever heard her voice, come to think of it. There were some troubled folks, no doubt. You could even have called her sinister, looking back. Nobody had a surname, and some didn't have real names at all.

That night I talked to two Irish brothers, Enda and Brian. Enda had plans for migrating, getting out of Ireland; he'd landed a job offer abroad, and this was their final fling, as Brian put it, and they intended to have a good time of it on this trip, come hell or high water. They had joined up with Big Red, a Canadian about six feet five with broad shoulders, in a cut-off lumberjack shirt. The seats on the Magic Bus were murdering his legs. He had a girlfriend back in Toronto and he went on incessantly about her, about staying true, and said he was going to make it official when he got back. And he told us how his dad ran a bar in Toronto called McKenna's and we would all get free beers there if we ever pitched up and mentioned his name. And many years ago, when I had the opportunity to go to that city, to my niece's wedding, I stood in the snow on a Toronto side street and looked at the red lights flashing, just an ordinary little sports bar with TV screens showing ice hockey. And I wanted very much to go inside, to ask for Big Red, but I couldn't bring myself to, not after everything that happened, so I never did find out if he stuck with that lucky girl.

Anton spoke to a waiter in a language which sounded like it could be plausible Turkish, no less. Clever old Anton! And the man brought us a plate of golden chips and skewered meat, with roasted peppers. We decided to stay a few days and before long it was agreed (or at least Fred arranged it and then told us) that we'd go along with the Magic Bus, follow the same route, though Anton told me quietly he thought we'd be doing at least fifteen miles an hour faster than that benighted bus, and if they broke down we jolly well weren't going to wait for them. A good Fred Trick, he said, is to make him think it's his idea.

We slept in the rooms above the restaurant that night, and in the morning I returned downstairs to the Pudding Shop because I didn't know anywhere else in Istanbul to go, hadn't developed the courage just to walk in the streets freely as if they were open to me. I knew enough to pull a thin scarf over my head. A lot of the chicks didn't bother, or went wandering off in shorts, and that upset me, because I heard the muttering and the way the local guys weren't too impressed. Don't worry about it, they like looking at our chicks' tits, said an Australian guy called Bob when I mentioned this in the Pudding Shop. It was true, the women got ogled, brought it on themselves, obviously, running around in bikini tops and parading like Miss World up and down Istiklal. I learned quickly how to make myself respectable.

In the morning, the café looked less daunting with natural grey light filtering through the glass shopfront. The waiters were charitable, and the toilets at the back weren't too bad, and had hot running water. I washed my face and cleaned my teeth. Outside the bathrooms was a closed glass booth with long-distance dialling and a pinboard covered in notes. White squares pinned with tacks, or gaps where the tacks had been prised out and re-used. People separated, lost to each other, abandoned. Malcolm to Megan, I'm sorry about the business down in Crete. Others parted, now living parallel journeys, if you see this we've taken the Black Sea route. What use would they be if you really lost someone?

The hippie with the red bandana and the dirty blonde dreadlocks, the one who had been sitting in the restaurant the night before, was looking at the board too, and he adjusted another message to make space for his own. I saw you coming in that four-by-four. A Manchester accent. He had a note in his hand and upside down I could read that he wanted a lift to India. The note was scrawled, terrible handwriting, as if he'd missed some essential weeks at school. Where are you heading? he asked. Our destination was Kathmandu, not that I wanted to reveal that to him.

Fred had a thing about getting to the Himalayas, his heart was set on the Annapurna range. There's a pink light in the mountains, they look like rose quartz at dawn, he'd say. He'd picked up grand ideas from the travellers he'd met back in Corfu on the beach; they'd told him some fancy words about the ranges in the morning, how every edge, every surface of those mountains is sculpted as if someone made them from glass and ice and diamonds, the pinkest sky and the whitest mountains, the rays burnishing each glacier. Makes you believe there's a God, that was the kind of thing Fred would say.

The hippie – he said his name was Chandra – had a little penny whistle tucked under his arm and a knapsack, barely enough to subsist on, and God knows we didn't need another musician. He was barefoot. I've done this trip before, I know the road like the back of my hand, man. I know a lot of groovy places to hang out. I'll give you guys a steer. Wow, Kathmandu, you have some revelations ahead, first time in the mountains man, what a trip. He said Chandra meant moon, and I was under no illusion that it was his real name.

I knew that Anton was worried about the van, that we were living on a wing and a prayer and he was already discussing spare parts, and I'd heard him say it might be good to have another person on board, to push and heave Vera out of a pothole, or to save us from whatever mechanical crises laid in wait. But I didn't want to share the back seats with this Chandra fellow; I knew he was bad news immediately. I was looking out for my boys, you see, and I didn't want anyone else getting in the way. We haven't got room, I said, and straightened a note on the pinboard. He looked at me and the way my fingers were working out a staple from the cork surface. Very well, he nodded, just let me know what day you're leaving. Put some shoes on, man, I thought.

Anton was in his element in Istanbul. I couldn't always keep up with his patter, to be honest, but I let him play the tour guide, sometimes he did whitter on, but he loved taking me around. Fred just doesn't get it, Anton said, he doesn't have the concentration span. It's good to have you with us. The following afternoon he took me on the ferry to a village called Eyup, it was just us and pilgrims, the women in headscarves pulled tight round their earnest faces. And that place, it wasn't just a mosque, it was a whole little world in itself. All the trinket sellers in the markets, prayer beads on both sides of the path until we reached the shrine, and graveyards, where a friend of the Prophet was encased in a tomb, and I followed the ladies in through the courtyard, and watched them stand with their hands together, as they asked for... what? Babies, safe deliveries, good marriages to solid men. I cupped my hands too, and on the way out Anton ran his hand along the turquoise tiles and told me about where the potters had lived and fired these shades of blue. I saw you praying, he said nosily. I asked for the journey to Kathmandu to go smoothly, I lied. I couldn't face telling him that I had more in common with those Turkish ladies in their headscarves than with him.

Anton's ordered ways were at odds with the mayhem of the road. He carried stacks of index cards, filed alphabetically and bound with rubber bands. Each one had meticulous lists of vocabulary in his tiny handwriting.

I found his habits reassuring, as if he was imposing order on us all. So I tried to pick up fragments, and to improve myself. I'd make an effort to listen to him when he gave impromptu lectures on the history of the Persian language. It had nudged out Arabic across a whole swathe of the world, he said, and even though it took on different forms, and they even called it Farsi instead of Persian in Afghanistan, really it was one language which had spread right across from the Ottomans to the Pashtuns to the Mughals who set up camp in India. I can admit, I learned a lot from Anton. He was, I still think, even taking into consideration everything that happened after that, a good person to travel with.

6

That night, when we returned from our visit to Eyup, Fred had left a note. He'd made some friends from West Berlin. We could find them at the Old City Palace hotel. When we arrived, Fred was in a courtyard at the back, sitting on a wall with three Spanish girls in headbands, placing a bright flower in the hair of one of them. More for the convoy, mates! he said excitedly. These guys are leaving for Tehran on Tuesday too, welcome to the show. And we're giving a lift to a fellow from Manchester called Chandra, alright, Anton? Anton shot me a doubtful look. The chap with the dreads? Actually, no, I don't think we should take that kid, Anton said, definitive. He looks flakey. Fred touched his arm. Don't be uptight, Antonios.

While we had been out sightseeing, Fred had been talking to everyone in the Pudding Shop – his currency was connecting up with people – and he'd met the red-bandana hippie. Who are the groupies? Anton said. One of the girls was leaning over Fred, her dress gaping. Ah, this is Marta, I think. That night the courtyard filled up with people, some of them I recognised already. Luxuriant moustaches, feathered headdresses, hats with wide brims and the odd fez. Fred pulled out his guitar and some girls in long dresses and scarves sat down around him, draping themselves like Pre-Raphaelite models, braless. And men gathered around too, in their fringed waistcoats, they didn't mind their girlfriends throwing themselves in such vulgar fashion at Fred, they just nodded along to the music. Big Red, the Canadian from the Magic Bus, produced a harmonica. We were all accompanying Fred.

Fred tapped his knee to keep time, and occasionally he'd pat the edge of the guitar so a hollow wooden sound rang out. The chords reverberated, and he made it look easy although I could see his right hand moving in convoluted patterns. He was hunched over the guitar, which gave him a bowed, penitent look. He didn't know how good he was, that's how it seemed. When he played he didn't look up, kept watch on his fingers, on the fretboard, and when we all whooped at the end his head was still bowed, he didn't straighten up or smile. Fred had a way of being the centre of attention and seeming like he didn't want to be. Your eyes went right to him.

After some time – I don't know how long he played for – he said, your turn, mister and lifted the guitar over his head, and handed it to the Irish lad Brian who fancied a strum.

I'm not feeling so good, said Anton, then, abruptly, I think I need to go. So I left the hotel with him and my last sight of Fred that night was him dancing, twirling two girls from Barcelona at once. Over the following days the floozies kept popping up, in the Pudding Shop and in the other restaurants we frequented, all kinds of chicks, and I guess he was picking them up and taking them back to his room. Curiosity about Fred was at a high at that point. He played up his plummy voice and one persistent story, all along the trail, was that he was a member of the royal family.

Fred could get on with anyone. And now, looking back, I think that drove a wedge between him and Anton; Anton had done all the correct reading, he knew the grammars of the local languages. But it was Fred who you'd find in the one-room shack of a taxi driver, with their baby on his lap. Or it was Fred who'd be given gifts by a local shopkeeper. Everything came easily to him because he emitted a sort of warmth – an easiness with the world, turning on his full-beam smile – which made other people feel like they could sit down beside him and unburden themselves. He sat with anyone he met on the trail for hours, junkies or mechanics, or boys who worked in the tea shack, teaching kids chords on the guitar. He didn't discriminate. And naturally, although he needed us, that could be hard to stomach if you were the jealous type.

Anton had the runs. Guts went to water. He wasn't a good patient, didn't even attempt to put a brave face on it. He bricked himself up in a single room, embarrassed about the stench. I was the one who checked in on him, found him a packet of rehydration salts in the first aid kit. Fred was too busy with his new mates, never even looked in on him, of course.

I had hardly known these men a month and now my days were structured by them, by their wishes and their feelings towards each other, their fevers and gut aches, the temperature of their friendship. It made me want to climb back into the van, Fred called it the inner sanctum, and return to the road. It was Sunday night and we were meant to leave on Tuesday. I was too scared or ignorant to go sightseeing alone and so I sat in the Pudding Shop, smoking and waiting for the boys to need me.

In the afternoon, Fred came in. He ordered Turkish coffee, which he ladled with heaps of sugar, and told me excitedly about an American he'd met the night before. You know he's a vet? Swear to God, I thought he meant something to do with animals. Got away from the front, went all wriggling through the jungle on his belly. Bullet in the head if they find him. The man is on the run. That's why he keeps going his own way. Fred was wearing a T-shirt with a slogan on it: *cada vida es preciosa*, which the Spanish chick named Marta had given him, it had been handed out to her at an anti-Vietnam demonstration in Barcelona, apparently. What does it say, I asked him? Every life is precious, he declared. I'm going to use it in a song, it's a great lyric, isn't it?

Fred's philosophies were hazy but there was something in them, I have to admit. Imagine, he said, a whole life, a whole person, who loves and is loved, just snuffed out, being there and then not being there, because you pulled the trigger? He made James Bond fingers, marvelling at the thought, at the ridiculous fragility of life, and how one person might end another's more easily than blowing out a candle. Instant karma's going to get you, he said. He was soaking up other people's ideas in those days, blending them into his hotchpotch creed.

I didn't have strong views on Vietnam, to be honest. My

parents were probably responsible for some of my opinions at the time, and so I might have said people were making too much of it, or it wasn't England's problem, Yanks getting themselves in a pretty pickle hardly warranted kids in London making a fuss with placards. My father held the view, I think it was quite common at the time, that the Americans didn't know how to fight Asiatics and they hadn't reckoned on guerilla warfare, foolishly ignoring British expertise. A young country without our experience in the tropics. I could tell Fred thought I was spouting borrowed drivel. He was a real peacenik; they're warmongers, hawks, butchers, he insisted. He agreed with me that America was a teenage country, like a young cowboy swaggering about after a night on the whisky. But he was simply against war, full stop. It was a different way of looking at the world, the peace dream, I'd never heard anyone spell it out in quite that way, mixing in Gandhian claptrap and John Lennon, and he really believed in peace, that we might be on the cusp of a serious world change. The details weren't well worked out but, I have to hand it to him, his faith was strong. Even the vicar is against Vietnam, back in Gloucestershire, he insisted. Joyce, honestly, it isn't a radical view anymore.

So what about this fourth seat in the van? he stirred the coffee. We'll take Chandra, right? You seriously want to give him a lift? I asked, and deliberately arched my eyebrows. *Naturellement*, said Fred, lighting a cigarette, it would be seriously uncool not to. Do you think Anton will mind? Well, we will have a majority of two, he said, counting on my vote. He hadn't seemed to notice my expression at all, or the fact that I hated the idea of Chandra joining us. To be frank, Fred could be very self-centred and, blimey, could he get his own way. You can break it to him. You're getting on better with Anton these days, aren't you? he said. Do you fancy him? The cheek. I said I honestly didn't, although perhaps I was unable to convey how I felt about him. I wanted to be liked by him. That was different. All the girls fancy Anton, he went on. Rich, coming from Fred. He's a handsome boy but I have to tell you – you're barking up the wrong tree, darling. Excuse me? He's a friend of Dorothy's. I tried not to disguise my shock. What would my parents have said! And on reflection, the news confirmed everything I'd already felt between me and Anton; the sense that we bore no threat to each other. He wasn't like other men, who seemed to have ulterior motives, to be operating on twin tracks, working out in their minds the statistical likelihood of sex.

I saw Anton in a new light too, remembered our first night, when he came back much later, after dark, having gone off to buy something, the sense that he was watching the movements of the waiters and the taxi drivers and the other travellers. His general unease matched with a confident bodily poise, a walking contradiction. A shameful secretiveness which life had forced on him. I tried not to judge him, even though I'd never met a homosexual before in my life. Open your mind, Joyce, I told myself. I liked Anton too much to let his predilections get in the way. I must say I was quite ahead of my time in that regard. I love him, but I don't fancy him, Fred said, stubbing out his cigarette in the ashtray. We never did it, even at boarding school.

Anton was feeling better, colour had returned to his cheeks and, although he still sighed and said his legs felt wobbly, he was anxious to get on the road again. Istanbul was a vortex that risked sucking us in, he said. The countryside beyond seemed vast; people warned us this was our last chance of Gauloises, and spare van parts, and music cassettes. Crossing from the European shore was a breach, another loosening from the moorings of home.

The last night in Istanbul, Fred announced we should splurge, and that he'd treat us to a night out in a superior hotel. Anton demurred at the last minute, he still wasn't feeling up to it, and so I went with Fred alone. The evening was balmy. The bar was lit low, with lanterns which gave it an illicit air, the feel of a speakeasy. Most of the clientele were Turkish, it wasn't a stoner's place. We sat on couches close to the ground. The waiter, lumbering and professional in a black waistcoat and bowtie, brought us a bottle of raki. I didn't know what it was and watched Fred, like an alchemist, turn the drink cloudy, using little tongs to mix in ice into a tall, thin glass. Try it, he said. It was hot liquorice and soothing, and I sipped it too fast, so I found later on, that when we stood up to return to our rooms, somehow my legs weren't fully reliable. Fred traced his fingers ever so slowly along my inner wrist. Why don't you unwind Joycie? he said. You're always watching us all, as if you're taking notes.

Here, said Fred, and he held my hand, like a lover, weaving his fingers between mine, and we walked back through the streets of Istanbul, back towards the Pudding Shop. He hummed as we walked, led me so gracefully, without even looking me in the eye, as if it was the most natural thing in the world for me to be guided to his room. His fingers were cool and long and the pressure on my own hand was just enough to convey seriousness of purpose. And then the spell broke, by his door, before he had produced a key. I looked at him and laughed. Frederick, don't even think about it, and I pecked him on the cheek, in the way that wives did to patronise their husbands. It was a passion-killing kiss. I walked down the corridor without looking back.

And you might ask, you might wonder, why was I so buttoned up? I thought a lot about Fred that night. The bed was hard, a mattress lain over a plank, and the heat, though nothing compared to what would follow, was new to me; I hadn't learned how to settle myself, and I didn't know how to sleep under a single sheet, anything other than heavy blankets, which was how I had slept all my life up until that point. A single sheet made me feel vulnerable and bare. The raki had left my throat dry.

And I thought about Fred and his songs, and his immense, undeniable talent – the timbre of a voice which could work on strangers like that – which seemed to me more exciting than anything I had seen in Istanbul, as monumental as any building. It was inevitable that a man like that was going to be flawed. I knew I shouldn't go there, but I wasn't going to let that stop me from watching him closely. I felt that between us there could be some sort of understanding, that perhaps by being the only woman who didn't sleep with him, I would make myself indispensable. I had the seed of an idea: I could help him to become great. And then he might realise how much he needed me. I wanted him to sing for his living and I wanted to make his dreams into a reality. If I was wrong on all these counts, then it was because I had bitten off more than I could chew. Fred wasn't willing to be tamed and he never knew just what was best for him. More fool me.

7

Our crowd, our caravan, had settled into some sort of floating population by the end of September. Needless to say, Fred won out, and Chandra joined us in the Land Rover. Anton didn't say another word about it and Chandra settled in next to me. We were driving behind the West Berliners in their VW, middle-aged ravers who had a taste for younger girlfriends, or lovers or wives. I was never sure who was the partner of who, or what precisely went on in that rainbow bus. Ahead of them, Aussie Bob, alone in his smart little car, who had been living in London, po-faced, had given up his job with IBM on a whim, thrown in the towel, said he was out of the rat race, but never stopped talking about the future of microcomputers. And of course, at the rear, the Magic Bus, the unreliable Bedford, driven by poor, worried Harjit-in-a-turban, with Big Red the Canadian on board and Tattoo Face and the Irish lads. And all the rumours and stories of folks who weren't even there, those who had gone before us, travelling ghosts, like eight-fingered Eddie, an Armenian who might have started out in Mexico but was living down in Goa; he helped stranded freaks and had set up a soup kitchen in Anjuna.

The Irish lads were irrepressible, daft in sheepskin coats and oversized sunglasses. Everyone was posturing, looking out for their interests, and for what they might get for themselves. Even in arid, vast places, we felt unconquerable, like we could just apply our pounds or dollars and a bit of English banter and we'd be able to work ourselves out of the stickiest spots, you know? And frequently we did. Everyone knew the story of how someone called Johnny Basildon had taught Turkish policemen Beatles songs and how they'd let him go when he'd got into bother near the border, kilos of the stuff sitting in his rucksack like Kendal mint cake.

And Good Lord, the freedom! Nowadays when you think about travelling Afghanistan or Iran you think of – what? – hostile armies, war zones, morality police, hardcore revolutionaries, Taliban nutters. You can't even do that journey anymore – not since 1978, once the Iranians kicked off – and the year after that the Russians went into Afghanistan. Honestly, did they think they could win against those fellows? Pull the other one. We just floated through, free as birds. A couple of times we had to wait for hours to get across a border, but there was never any question of not getting across. Those places had their own problems, as they still do today, but things were so much better back then, you understand – we were so free! It was a doddle! A few westerners in raggedy clothes passing through were the least of their worries.

So policemen turned a blind eye, let us float on by. We were pesky irritants, as minor as mosquitoes, or maybe even welcome in some places where we spent our meagre cash. Quite a few savvy locals got rich on the back of understanding quickly how to cook up banana pancakes. When I looked at the map and saw the line we were making I felt proud of being able to roll across the world from one side to the other; it seemed like an achievement in itself.

No one had any past or future; it wasn't the done thing to ask too much. You never got a surname, just a vague sense of where people came from: a city, a country, perhaps an occupation if someone was being particularly nosey. Cheeky bugger. That was enough to shut anyone up. Evading answers, cultivating mystery. We had all reinvented ourselves a little, and that was the fun of it, playing at being reckless until we really became wild. So the three of us, Fred, Anton and I, had a kind of compact – silently – not to reveal what we knew about each other, to keep things under our belts. As if it's that easy to take off your history. From my experience, getting rid of your past is as easy as taking off your underwear. It's the consequences you need to worry about.

We headed towards Ankara, and I had been right. Our new passenger, Chandra, was utterly impractical, a waste of space, to be honest. Not surprising, really, in retrospect. He couldn't recall anything about the road or recommend where to stay and he was skint as a church mouse. He sat there uselessly while Fred and Anton did simple things like pouring water into the radiator. Anton jacked up the car in quick time when we got a flat, using blocks of wood and spanners, patching it up well while Chandra sat cross-legged on the roadside as if he might levitate his way to India. On the upside, he never asked for anything, and for hours he barely spoke. When we stopped at a roadside canteen, he looked at the menu carefully, chose plain rice, ate it in slow, regular mouthfuls. That would do him for another day. He refused shared snacks, drank the local tap water, scooping it up with his hands. He didn't want to depend on anyone, which was daft seeing as he was completely depending on us to get him across eight hundred miles of Turkey.

Anton tried a few times, in his way, and extracted pieces of information: he was from Manchester, he'd dropped out of school very young, then dropped out of art school, and then dropped out of Manchester. He'd been to India twice before but now he was planning to stay for what he described, with a serious face, as eternity. Mostly he looked out of the window, sick if I read, he said when I waved a newspaper at him which was out of date in any case. He pressed his forehead against the window or he sprawled out, sharing his spliff with Fred, leaning across the gearstick to hand it over, and nodding his head to the music, Bob Dylan on a loop.

I have to admit, I could barely tell some of the freaks apart. Their faded orange clothes and their ratty beards and their impregnation of dope made them all look the same; maybe the drugs were fusing them all into the universal after all, maybe they really were losing their egos. Fred said we were priggish making these distinctions, that we were all on the road together. Travellers, freaks, what the hell is the difference? You might be being a teensy bit judgemental, Joyce, he said. When we stopped for tea or snacks he would always buy something for Chandra; Fred had old-school chivalry, granted.

Chandra would stare at me as we sat at those roadside shacks, and it made me uncomfortable, not in a boobs and bum way, but as if he was sizing me up, spiritually. As if he was checking if I measured up to some divine criteria. He claimed he could read auras and could see the colours in a halo, radiating around my body. Your aura is dark, Joycie, he said, one afternoon by a roadside canteen, as we sipped black tea, there's a lot of negative energy around you. And I don't mind telling you, that riled me. The cheek of it! Karma this, and karma that; it was a canny way of not taking responsibility for yourself in my book. All that mumbo jumbo. And there by the roadside, he offered me the roach from his grubby little fingers, which I refused, and he shook his head in disappointment. You've got to lighten up, Joyce, seriously. He exhaled deeply. You need to connect with your inner child. We all have a frightened inner child, Joyce. I became even more determined then to never let that journey change a thing about me, not one iota.

What are you actually going to do in India, Chandra? Anton asked one day as he changed the radio to a station playing Ravi Shankar. I am seeking liberation, Chandra said, because I sure as hell don't want to come back to this world for another life. There was an ashram in Poona, he'd shacked up there for a while the previous year, and that's where he was returning, to see his guru. He'd gone back to England to tie up some loose ends, as he put it.

I guess it was somewhere on the outskirts of Ankara, ugly endless blocks of flats, Soviet in appearance, that the police stopped us for the first time. Fred was behind the wheel. The policeman flagged us down; he had little orange plastic cones which they'd set up in the road. What a baby face, Fred said, and Anton hushed him. He did have a sweet round face, a light fluff on his upper lip, and we couldn't quite take him seriously, despite the gun on his holster. You see, it was all a big game in those days, at the beginning of the overland. He wanted to take down our details, the car registration, and our passport numbers on a form.

Chandra, can you fill this in? Fred passed across the form while the policeman stood sweating in the heat by the side of the van. Chandra held the pen in his hand, lifted it up, chewed the lid. Pressed it to the paper, made a mark with all the hesitancy of a child. He had ways of dodging pen to paper. Letters circling like sharks in the water. Fred took the pen and filled it in for all of us without a second of hesitation.

We should have feared the police with moustaches and big guns and strange uniforms who looked deadly serious; not exactly bobbies on the beat. He asked us, through the window, if we were carrying any drugs, and he seemed to look most pointedly at Chandra. We all denied anything, of course, what else was there to do? Then Fred did the barmiest thing, one of the stories we told again and again on the road. He said in his most regal voice, Officer, I am so sorry, it's true I do have a small quantity of narcotics on my person. And he handed over a tiny, microscopic-sized piece of hashish in a paper wrap.

Everyone in the van was quiet as the policeman rotated the tiny piece over in his hands as if he'd been handed a grenade, as if he would have rather hurled it away into the lay-by. Fred had created a problem for him now. We also all knew that he'd saved us hours of searching and unpacking – and possibly worse if they'd found Fred's real stash, which was more substantial. I don't know, looking back, perhaps it was a trick that Fred had been told about in the Pudding Shop, a ruse that the experienced passed on.

Eventually, after the silence had stretched out interminably, the policeman said, alright, on you go, good journey, and waved us forwards past his little orange cones. We hadn't been busted. We were laughing and cheering, refining the anecdote as we went on towards Ankara.

Chandra hadn't said a word, and then as we pulled into Ankara he said, can you let me down here, folks? He was irrationally scared of getting nicked, you see, absolutely couldn't handle what had happened. Come on, Chandra, we'll take you as far as the hostel in Ankara, Fred said. I can't be mixing with this, got to kick loose, guys. Not my thing. You've been good. No jokes with cops, though. No can do. He relented in the end, sat in his usual silence, tapping his fingers against the door handle; he couldn't wait to get shot of us, as if he was on the run. Listen, he said, finally. I had a friend who got busted in Bombay and I went to visit him, and I can tell you, I never smelled anything so rotten in my life. That smell, like the shittiest sewer, and the guy reeked, he just smelled of layers of old crap. I took him gifts but he never even said thank you, just asked again and again for money, grabbing onto me and pleading like some kind of medieval peasant, because he was so far gone on smack. It was a shame, because he hadn't been that way before he went inside. It was twisted.

The next morning, when we gathered together for

breakfast, Chandra had gone. It was as if he had never existed. Some of the Magic Bus folks said he'd found a seat on a different bus; others said that he got a ride with another van. No note or letter of explanation. The West Berliners assured us he might have been meditating, or off his head, or both, and there was another rumour that he'd hitched on the back of a motorbike with someone we'd never heard of and would follow in a few more days. Good riddance, I said, he gives me the heebie-jeebies. I didn't want to take lessons in spirituality any longer from that crusty fellow with his unwashed clothes and his half-baked ideas. I didn't trust Chandra as far as I could throw him. But Fred said, don't be such a square, Joyce, in a rather hurt voice, and it was obvious that he thought rather a lot more of him than I would have expected. I believe I remember Fred saying something like, Chandra's a pretty wise dude, without a doubt, he's got a lot of insight. That settled the matter, and Anton and I were not allowed to question his judgement any further. And today, you'll agree, as time proved, how right I was to try and keep that grimy pothead away from Fred. If only he had listened to me, and to Anton, instead of thinking he could have everything his own way.

8

There were two roads and a choice from Ankara:
northwards on the Black Sea, or inland to Nevsehir in
Cappadocia, and we followed the Magic Bus inland
towards Nevsehir, and its moonscape. We rolled into the
town in the late afternoon. The family homes we'd heard
about, which would once take you in for free, had grown
into guest houses. A man who'd got ahead of the game was
having a second storey constructed on his house in the new
town, and people talked about how the concrete mixer ran
night and day. They lavished us with food, melons and
cheese and bread, and then demanded money. One or two
of the earnest young men who read newspapers and spoke
English got into a debate with Anton about the defeat
of Harold Wilson the previous summer. I wasn't one for
politics, but I knew that was good riddance. The kids were
getting wise to extracting items from westerners too. One
coin. One pen. Crafty. They could pull the right attitude for
pictures, and Fred leapt about with them, egging them on,
encouraging them to beg, really. There was a joke doing

the rounds in Nevsehir, about a Turkish man painting a donkey to sell it back to his father. They overcharged us to sleep in rooms cut out of caves, natural hollows, without windows.

When I woke the next morning it was silent, and then I heard swearing. I couldn't tell if it was day or night and felt scared for a minute to think of myself in this desert so far from anything familiar. It was Fred, he'd slipped with nail scissors, cut his nail perilously close to the cuticle, so the nailbed had filled with blood. He was panicking. Shit. Here, let me help you. I grabbed my first aid bag and took a length of plaster from it, snipped it then gently pushed the sticky end over the tip of his finger. All the time Fred held out his long-fingered hand passively, looking away. Cannot stand the sight of blood, he said. It was not a serious wound, and I was pleased to be of use. I've never been a squeamish person. Oh, I'm a baby about blood, Fred said, blame the hunt.

He told me then, something that I've never forgotten after all these years, how when he was about five or six, feeling like a little man, he was taken out for the first time. How his father jostled him to the front so he could see the kill; the dogs ripping the fox to shreds. And then how the leader of the hunt picked up the tail of the fox, sliced it clean away from the carcass and beckoned him down from his pony. And now I'm standing in a clearing with the men high above me, he said, in their scarlet jackets, up on saddles. And the leader dips the tail in the blood of the fox, still warm, holds my face up and smears three lines on it, across my cheeks and my forehead. Fred said he felt sick but he was meant to smile because all the men around him, led by his father, were cheering and the huntsman was blowing the horn and they were passing around a cup of sloe gin. So I smiled and tried not to wipe away the blood, which was drying on my skin, as he talked he rubbed his face as if wiping away that moment, and then we rode back to the house and as soon as I could I escaped to the lav. He looked at me and laughed, oh well, tally-ho – he'd been ladling on the melodrama. And that, my dear, is why I *cannot* stand the sight of blood. I packed away the roll of plaster and removed the other signs of blood as quickly as I could, crumpling up the tissue with red stains on it, aware that Fred could be hurt simply by the sight of something that runs in us all.

But that was Fred's family custom, wasn't it? He was turning his back on all that tradition. Hunting was part of his inheritance, after all. Generations of Carruthers had been riding to hounds. He went on and on about animals. And the vegetarianism! I knew that he'd been sticking to the vegetarian thing in a rigid way, with discipline, completely contrary to the way he smoked pot. Waving away plates in restaurants, inspecting the lumps under curry sauce with his fork, as if looking for a lost insect. He had it all worked out about meat, his thoughts about animal consciousness sounded like hocus-pocus to me, if I'm honest, though I didn't dare say that to Fred.

I clearly recall one other incident along that section of the road around that time, at a pit stop between Kayseri and Sivas. Bugger of a day, said Anton. The Magic Bus in front ground to a halt, and we all followed suit. Somehow we were never on our own for long, even though I craved having the boys to myself, and Anton had sworn we wouldn't wait on the Magic Bus. It just kind of happened. Fred always found a way into the slipstream of other travellers, he was suited to a crowd.

The passengers climbed down in sickly silence, Big Red complaining about the tiny seats, limbering up his back. The Irish lads still trying their utmost to piss about, in spite of the mood. Harjit the driver had bags under his eyes, a look of pure exhaustion across his brow, worried about the responsibility of getting his passengers from A to B. I took a piss as best I could behind a bush. Others sipped water from the flasks or something stronger from a hip flask and tanked up the gallons. People sat on the stony earth or bumpers, eating apples, looking as if they'd walked there, not been carried in vehicles.

I was aware of Aussie Bob peering at Anton, who was unfolding on the bonnet a large-scale map which was worn through at the folds. Fred was standing to his left, pretending to be interested in the route. Hey, Fred, I've just noticed, Bob called out, hasn't your mate got a touch of the tar brush? Bob was looking at Anton, inspecting him again as if he had just seen him. Bob beckoned to me. Hey, whad d'you think, princess? I was arranging my clothes.

I suppose Anton was the colour that people politely call olive. I heard a girl rave about his tan, how lucky he was to brown like that, not needing to fuss over peeling and burning and messy lotions. Anton seemed not to hear and carried on peering at the map. I didn't know what to say so I shrugged, offhand, and drank my water. Bob didn't let things drop that easily. Hey, do you think that's just a tan? he said to Fred, as if he'd discovered some dangerous family secret. Anton had gone very still and continued reading the map. Could pass for a local, mate.

Bob, Fred said, and his voice sounded classy, do you want to be in a race? Bob nodded back, confused, ready for a challenge, whatever Fred was throwing down. Well, come on then, you can join the human race, Fred said. He went and stood by Anton's side and they looked at the map together, even though Fred couldn't have cared less about the route; in fact, Fred was the worst navigator I ever met. Aussie Bob had got me thinking though about Anton's family tree, where he was *really* from. His full name was Antonios Aziz, for real, it wasn't a joke. Anton once said his family were Coptic Christians. Nowadays the whole of England seems to be full of these types, we're meant to call them mixed race, aren't we? But back then, I heard my mother's voice in my head; fancy that, our Joyce travelling the world with an Arab, a homosexual Arab, at that. And I did check out Anton's skin, when he wasn't looking, and wondered what dark secrets lay in his family tree. I didn't like to pry after that, though, not after the way Fred had looked daggers. When we got back in the van, Fred said, fucking Aussie Bob, damn cheek.

The pair of them stood up for each other if there was ever any external threat, like cubs from the same litter. I always respected that; it was one of the things I most admired about their relationship. It's a rare thing indeed, I don't think I've ever had that kind of shield, someone you can rely on to defend you like a praetorian guard. When you live alone, as I have always done, you must become used to protecting yourself.

★

The mood in the van altered, became more serious, on the final leg of Turkish road. Anton tuned into Sufi music, and we settled in for long, uncomfortable hours. Old men herding sheep along the roadsides stared at us uncertainly, and children chased us, throwing pebbles at the van, laughing. The road ran parallel to derelict railway track and there was only one way to drive along the ravine. We'd stop for the boys to take a leak, or just to shake out our legs.

Then the road degenerated. We were forever getting lost on those endless plains. Occasionally a tank with Turkish soldiers would roll by and young men with buzz cuts would nod at us. Just ask them the way, Fred would say. Are you mad? Anton would always reply. The direction was east, we couldn't go too far wrong. We were climbing upwards, which was hard on the van. Sand crunching like sugar underneath the tyres. We willed her on and, one way or another, we reached Dogubayazit.

It was too cold to sleep outside, so we slept as best we could in the van under bags and blankets. The temperature plummeted at night in those parts. In the morning I woke to see the slopes of Mount Ararat from the window of the van, monumental and dormant, white snow contrasting with the ocean of brown land around us. I thought of royal icing, set crunch-hard into sugary peaks on a wedding cake. I felt a long way from everything I'd fled.

Fred was standing outside, inhaling, getting through his stockpile before the border. Anton was shaving, tilting his chin at the wing mirror. Not far from Dogubayazit, we crossed from Turkey to Iran. A little hut and a pink customs house; the border guards put on a show, prodding Fred's open chest, holding up his necklace, smiling all the time. He joshed with them a bit and they patted him on the back. Up in the hills long caravans of tanks snaked around, artillery with mounted guns facing each other across the pass. Russians on the horizon. Anton's mind was in the past, he didn't seem to care about the soldiers. Persia, Anton said, rolling the word on his tongue. I am only ever going to call it Persia.

PART 3

PERSIA

9

Somewhere near the Tehran border we did a cash count, with a view to changing lira for Iranian tomans. We were standing round the van and spread our remaining money and traveller's cheques out in front of each other on a small camping table. Anton peeled his out from a travel purse he wore tightly buckled around his waist. It makes you look like a pussy, Fred said, who kept coins and notes loosely in different places, in his pockets or stuffed in the side of his backpack. Give it a rest, Fred. Anton whacked him with the money belt. Fred put him in a headlock and ruffled his hair, and they were puppies again, laughing, rolling on the floor.

It turned out I had a lot less dosh than I'd expected. We'd all been spending more than we should have been. Constant tea, meals in restaurants. Not a lot, nothing really fancy, locally speaking. I mean, when did I take a taxi back home? If I saw something in the market that I wanted, something small like a ring or a scarf, it was mine. I hardly had to say no to myself. Besides, most items were cheaper than back home, and often they seemed laughably cheap, ridiculous even, and that was another reason to rush towards India, because there the rate of the rupee to pound was legendary. Around that time I started collecting my lovely little bits and pieces. I had started wanting objects, that's the truth. I had this urge to collect beautiful things, and I couldn't stop myself from picking up *objets d'art* from market stalls. I think it started with some Iznik tiles, nothing too fancy, you understand. Some of the items were unique – it's all different nowadays, you can get your mitts on anything with all this internet shopping, but we just didn't have those sorts of things to buy back home. And I burned for them, I would wake up thinking of something I'd seen in the marketplace.

Anton was worried, though. Going to have to go steady, sticking to a daily budget, he said. Go easy on the shopping, Joyce. Don't worry, we'll be alright, Fred reassured him. Anton was restraining himself, I knew, from saying, well, it's easy for you to say, Fred. He was the only one of us who was underwritten. Anton couldn't turn to home either and that raised the stakes, made our budgeting a critical matter. He sounded just like Fred – their voices rubbed to a shine by school debates and chapel readings – but Anton had it harder. He never pretended to the same wealth as Fred, and he was careful on the overland, tucking away his change, haggling politely when we went to buy necessary things like fuel, or soap, or tea. Fred would just hand over the coins, or notes, whatever was demanded, cheerfully astonished when he got change.

I asked Fred about Anton's family one day when I had the chance. We'd parked up for a night, and Anton was studying. He liked to sit on an old tartan travel rug on the grass, with a book on his knee. Fred and I wandered down to a stream at the far side of a gorge. Anton's old pops, well he was just a nice GP. Nothing too special. Fred skimmed a stone, making it bounce on the water. So where did he get such a foreign name? I pressed. Fred looked shifty, ask him yourself, he said. But then he told me anyway, that Dr Aziz had been born in Egypt, came to London for his medical training and got the hots for an Englishwoman. He was a dapper little man, with a taste for pickles from Fortnum's. Anton grew up in an apartment just off Kensington High Street. Anton's father had worked hard, swore allegiance to the NHS after the war. But for some reason, perhaps a lack of ambition – that was Anton's mother's theory – he was never given a position in a hospital. For years he'd slogged away as a GP, getting frustrated by his lot. Then when Anton was still at school, in a moment of sudden energy, he'd set up a private practice on Harley Street. Road to Damascus, said Fred, spent everything on the consulting rooms, on gilt-edged cards, a foxy receptionist. The patients didn't turn up in the expected numbers, and within months he was declared bankrupt. I'm sorry, the headmaster said, we are not a charity. That's when my father stepped in, said Fred, looking down at a stone in his palm.

And when only a few months later, Anton's dad keeled over with heart failure, at sixty-five, and his mother took charge of the accounts, it came to light that Dr Aziz's expenditure had been even more outrageous than they'd thought over the years. He'd had a penchant for casinos. His debts tripled and quadrupled before their eyes, and it confirmed that the earl had done the right thing, and his responsibility for the boy was sealed.

And now and then, Fred's father would say to him, proudly, Anton's such a gifted boy, forgetting that he was speaking to his own son, forgetting all the imbalances between them, and so Anton and Fred's relationship was like a seesaw, you understand, wired on an axis of money and privilege, unstable and risky. Anton was only ever a guest at the big house, he'd never inhabit it. Could marry one of my sisters, Fred said once, when they were discussing the future. I reckon one of them would have you. Unlikely, isn't it? said Anton. Well, you wouldn't be the first or the last queer in the family.

We all needed to save money and we fancied the break and it seemed like such a good solution. Freddie hadn't gone into great detail, that wasn't his forte. He'd promised food and comfortable beds. Family friends, possibly godparents, though the relationship was hazy. Sir Guy and Aunt Patricia – or Aunt Trixie – had been in Tehran for donkey's years, and they would definitely have every kind of booze. That was all we had to go on. Can't bloody well go through Tehran without bloody well stopping off with us, that was the order. Sir Guy was military attaché to the embassy. Once I understood that we would be kipping in their private house, a nineteenth-century French villa off Pahlavi Street, I was quite nervous at the prospect of turning up on their doorstep. On the other hand, anything free had its attractions by this point, and I overcame my shame as I studied the dirt which had wedged between my toes below the rubber of my flipflops.

The street was long and elegant; we had become so used

to outskirts, parking across the tracks, that it was a shock to roll right into the centre of that long avenue lined with plane trees, and to see the tailors' shops and tea rooms, and the college girls in flares linking arms. The door was ten feet high and surrounded by blue enamel tiles. A maid answered, black-and-white frills all over.

Aunt Trixie shrieked with joy when she saw Fred. She had tears in her eyes when she held him away from her and looked at him. Then she murmured words to the maid – towels, soap, baths. To her credit, she had become used to the sight of her friends' children wafting into and out of Tehran, part of her mission was to clean them up, feed them, dispatch them in good order. Perhaps she reported back to the parents, it was hard to know. She asked me my name twice, as if I was an extra number, although I had made sure that Freddie had telegraphed ahead from Erzurum. They rustled me up my own bedroom in any case, and the whitest towels I saw on the whole journey.

And those rooms. Gold-plated taps. Plump mattresses. A large mirror in which I saw myself at full length for the first time in several weeks, thinner and browner, all the sloppy food making me into a wiry version of the girl who had boarded the ship at Dover. But my hair was just the same; I got it cut by barbers along the road, didn't let it grow wild like the others. And there was something reassuring about my look. I hadn't changed as much as the boys, you see; I had zero intention of going native.

My room had a balcony and below the city lights were snapping on, Cadillacs and yellow taxis waiting bumper to bumper, and the men illuminated in the cafés, at their chess sets and narghiles, waiting for the next move. I eased myself out of my clothes and felt the water rise around me to my chin, the first and only time on that entire journey that I was submerged in a full tub.

I was tense around Aunt Trixie, about the thought of attending her party that evening. She wasn't a real aunt, Fred's mother's closest friend, it became apparent, they had grown up together in the same village. Unlike other acquaintances she hadn't ducked her illness, had been a steadfast visitor, had come every single day with flowers and gossip. She'd come up with the right words at the funeral, which had stuck in little Fred's mind, he said, Trix stood by us. And she knows how to mix a drink. We met on the landing, all steamed anew, giggled, and descended the stairs together, raising our eyebrows at the place. Freddie was running his fingers through his damp hair.

Well, don't you all look better? Aunt Trixie was in a drawing room lush with thick wallpaper and gilt mirrors which reached as high as the ceiling. She had a cigarette which dangled without real commitment in one hand, and she seemed entirely made up of the material all around her, the fabrics that draped from the windows and from her body, and the jewels on her fingers, so that when I tried to imagine her in shorts, on a beach, say, I found it completely impossible. I couldn't separate her from this room. Trixie was about as far from my own mother as a woman could be.

She looked at me, lifted one arm tentatively as if she wanted to adjust my hair. Freddie had tied his hair back and shaved, restored to some sort of schoolboy demeanour, and seemed a bit different around this adult who had known him since birth. He smoked a cigarette intensively, no chance of sneaking a reefer in this house, and reached towards a large crystal ashtray. It was very odd after weeks of bumping along in Vera. Cool house, said Freddie.

All I could see was the food. Trixie saw our faces and led us to the spread, insisted we eat and drink, said that this was the least she could do for intrepids like us, that we should treat the place as our own, fatten ourselves up so we would be fortified for the journey. She was so thrilled to have us, and Sir Guy came in at that moment, and strode towards us, and gave his wife a flamboyant kiss on both cheeks. They seemed so shimmering compared to everyone that I had met during the past weeks on the road that I couldn't really summon the right words and stood rather dumbly, looking on.

Trixie greeted everyone as they came in, glamourous people one after the other, and told jokes, and I couldn't help thinking they might be lines she had used before, perhaps many times before. You are going to tell everyone what a wonderful time you had with us. She was insistent we would have a great stay, maybe now I would say she was desperate to be loved. And she couldn't quite leave Freddie in peace, was always darting around him, as if he'd become the centre of the room.

I've seen my fair share of fancy houses now, and any number of antiques. Nowadays I'd know how to deal with her type. She thought I was insignificant, a little girl from the suburbs, and that she knew Fred best. But I was the one who got to be with Fred for weeks ahead, who would see him sleeping, and know his bowel movements and the contents of his rucksack. There was no way Trixie could compete with me. I mattered much more to Fred than she did. And I think, now, to be frank, the more she tried, the more she made Fred uncomfortable. You see, I already knew the best way to handle Fred. He hated dredging up all that stuff from the past, which is what Trixie kept trying to make him do. But these are probably thoughts that came later, when I reflected on that evening. I'm rushing ahead of myself.

Right, what have we here? Sir Guy pulled Freddie into a happy hug of welcome, and asked questions about the boys' old school, which he'd gone to before the war, and the cricket team, and Anton answered gamely. I could tell that Anton wanted, as always, to turn the conversation to politics and to draw Guy on the real substance, but he brushed off anything other than the most banal inquiry. Ah, the Shah, well, enemies at every gate, he muttered.

An Italian woman was kissing Trixie in greeting, and another English couple had arrived with their trench coats on their arms, less garrulous, on their first posting. The servant, a different person to the maid who'd drawn our baths, was bobbing from person to person, quickly refilling the glasses which were being refilled and drained and refilled before anyone had had enough food. An Iranian couple had a huddle around them, the woman astonishingly haughty in large sunglasses and pearl choker, some inches taller than the bloke.

Trixie had moved on, I noticed, from a martini glass to a champagne glass, although the cigarette still dangled at her side, and she stayed with our group. We hadn't mingled. Trixie looked at Fred with unconcealed adoration, having to restrain herself from touching him. She was making comparisons with his mother, even though it made him squirm. She'd last seen Fred when he was in the sixth form. Isn't he like her? she said to me, as if I could agree.

So how is your father, Freddie? And I don't just want a trite answer. I mean how is he, really? She seemed to have decided to include me and Anton in the inner circle, that we might be rolled together with Freddie – Freddie's chums – as one entity, privy to their conversations. God, it's years since I've seen him. She sounded wistful. Freddie was monosyllabic, shuffling from foot to foot – I guess the lack of harder substances was a factor. Anton said a few things about the earl in response, sparing Freddie. He filled Trixie in on the latest at the house, the repairs to the west wing, the revelation of the wall paintings which confirmed the date of that part of the building. She listened politely, he told a good tale, took us all into the gardens in our minds, drawing the drapes to the landscaped valley with the view of the lake.

After all that terrible business... I mean... he was just the messenger, just the man on the spot. Someone had to do it. What a time. I think that was the last straw for your mother. What you all went through in the colonies! Long nights and days he was gone, out to the camps in the jungle. I remember him telling me all about it. He deserves every medal they pin on him in my view. She spoke about Fred's father as if she owned him and there was some special claim she staked. A hit with the ladies, wasn't that Anton's phrase?

I was just a baby, Freddie mumbled cautiously, and I sensed that, if he could, he would have hummed or even broken into song. Anton inspected the colour of his wine, and his glass was filled instantly by the servant in baggy trousers with a pink sash. Freddie was looking around as if for a way to excuse himself, finding all the escape hatches closing, all the gateways being blocked off. Beastly, she mouthed the word, as if it might be dirty, then added another iteration more loudly and with confidence, beastly. I realised she was probably a bit worse for wear, the colour was rising in her cheeks, and finally she had the chance to say many things which she had been storing up for days.

And that dear man in the midst of it all, trying to seal off the capital, can you imagine? In the end they needed the RAF – like a war, wasn't it, Guy? She called him over for affirmation, it all came down to air power in the end, didn't it? Control of the skies, to knock out those rebel gangs in the jungle, and she puffed out a perfect ring of smoke as if recreating the trails left in the sky by a bomber. I was just a baby, Freddie said again. Anton heard him say this, and valiantly coughed, tried to change the subject. But Trixie was on a roll. We understood the choices one had to make, didn't we, unlike some others. Not easy at all dealing with that. He's a hero, Fred, you should be proud of him.

Trixie, Fred said, and those of us who knew him best heard the warning note in his voice. Trix, dearest heart, would you mind shutting the fuck up about all that.

I will tell you, I was stunned. If Fred had spoken to me like that I'd have slapped him hard across the face, and Anton gripped his arm as if he was going to lead him away. But these people were weird, they didn't mind foul language, they seemed to expect it. And Trixie just blinked her lashes, and smiled as if she hadn't heard a thing.

I'm sorry, my wife is up to it again. She loves to reminisce.

Patricia, these young people want to make hoopla, not talk about history. All long and gone, Freddie, no? And Guy put both hands on his shoulders and pulled him up straight, like a slouched soldier on the parade ground. Old history.

And then she turned to me, and she seemed not in the least bit flustered, in utter denial of Fred's words. Not met a nice young man of your own, my dear? If you ask me they're going the way of the steam train.

We stayed three or four nights. The boys were uncomfortable. Always the same in the evenings, lavish drinks and finger food, guests coming in and out. Trixie and Guy hadn't had children. Instead she looked after the whole world in her house. She worked, I decided, harder than Guy, remembering names, smoothing over details, issuing invitations. It was full-time, no doubt about it. Much to my disappointment, Trixie never raised the subject of the earl again. She and Guy stuck doggedly to safer subjects. Tiresome, even by the third night the party felt like a routine. And although it was all free, which was, no doubt, a bonus, Fred wanted to move on.

Anton was also ill at ease in the house. He was cross with Fred that night, told him not to be a wanker, that Trixie was just trying to be nice. But I could see he disapproved of them too, he was upset that they had all this time – the freedom of Tehran, the run of all the old archaeological sites – and they hadn't even tried to learn Farsi, he said more than once, and he couldn't believe Guy didn't know the poetry of a man who Anton revered, was always banging on about, and Fred told him to shut up, not everyone was an intellectual. Oh, do give it a rest, old love, he can read whatever he wants to read, let people do what they like. Maybe, I guess, looking back, it seemed like a goading. Maybe Fred felt that Anton was actually criticising him.

Those were the days of the Shah; Trixie and Guy attended the celebrations in the desert at Persepolis to mark two thousand five hundred years of the Persian empire, chaperoning the Duke of Edinburgh. I actually saw them on the television after I had returned to England, just a glimpse on the evening news. Distinctly Trixie, in a floral dress with her hair styled differently, blow-dried into a bouffant, and Guy leading her with an arm at the small of her back. People said it was the greatest banquet ever held in history, the commentators ran out of superlatives for the excess. Fifty thousand birds were flown in from Europe so that the guests would wake up to the sweet sound of songbirds in the morning, only they wilted and died in the desert heat, dropping off their perches. Not long afterwards came the Iranian revolution. Trixie and Guy had to flee in a hurry, I guess, and I sometimes wonder what happened to that excellent wine cellar, and imagine a greybeard ayatollah taking ownership of that house, soaking in the bathtub with the cherubs on the walls.

Fred brought Vera back from the embassy compound to the front door of the house and blasted the horn. Trixie came down the steps with bags of food for us to load in the back, wine, olives, cartons of expensive imported biscuits. She looked bemused by the van. She was sorry to see us go, especially Fred. She gave him a warm hug, kissing him on different cheeks, and said several times that he was in a better state than when he'd arrived. And look, she said, these are yours, you should have them, Freddie. She handed him a small brown-paper foolscap folder, kissed him again.

That parcel, I know now, was full of letters. That bundle wasn't precious to Fred, he treated the letters as badly as the rest of his stuff, and the folder was soon rumpled. But he didn't lose them, either. I caught sight of them now and again in the side pocket of his backpack; he kept them through all the ups and downs of the road, when even his passport was wrecked with water stains. I was longing to see what those letters contained, as if they might unlock Fred himself.

At some unfathomable level, I'd made a commitment to Frederick Carruthers by this point. I wasn't in love with him, of course. The stupidity of loving Fred was very clear, even to the wildest and – frankly – sluttiest girls on the trail. Not a rational proposition. I was merely keeping my promise to Anton to keep an eye on him. I had decided: I would watch over him, and I'd keep him on the straight and narrow. I would make sure he returned to England safely. And I can't explain it now any more than I could then. I will admit, even today, I have visions of him in the night. I still think of the things he would say and the way his melodies might strike a heart, and I'm not sure sometimes if I was captivated by him or by the sound he made on a guitar.

10

The road from Tehran to Mashad was straight and well tarmacked for seven hundred miles. A chain of small towns – Firuzkuh, followed by Semnan, Shahrud, Sabzevar. I have all the maps in front of me now, incredible what you can do with the help of Google Earth, how you can see those tiny little towns, a little string of beads across Asia, from the comfort of a desk in England. Such an aide memoire. We wanted to get out of Iran, move forward, didn't have patience for small places. Folks without their own vehicles caught the night train and, for the first time, we felt sorry to have our own wheels. Anton was resolute, took the lion's share. He said he would drive slowly through to dawn, with the lights off to preserve the battery. I remember the sight of vans, apple greens and reds, loaded with cargoes of food and fruit, the distances between villages becoming longer, before I drifted off to sleep.

I woke to a crunch. What's happening? Something wrong with the van, said Fred. The car had ground to a halt in the middle of the main road, on an isolated patch, far from any settlements. It was dark outside, nothing apart from the sounds of screeching owls, no lights in the distance, fields spreading into blackness on both sides. Anton was rooting around for the paraffin lamp, which he then held over the bonnet. Fred had gathered a blanket around his shoulders, and the two of them peered inside and I could tell from their faces they were worried, two soothsayers looking at the entrails. I felt a finger of fear reach out and touch me. Anton poked about inside the engine, while Fred took his turn to hold the lamp aloft, lighting up areas of the interior.

I think it's the clutch, Anton reported. The clutch had been one of the subjects of concern, on and off; sod's law it would go on our longest run of night driving. It might not be that, he admitted, it could be anything. Bummer. We were stuck there for the night, there was nothing to be done, no movement possible. Fred climbed into the back and he wrapped an arm loosely around me in a protective way, so I was swaddled tight and felt better than I had done for a long time. Don't worry, Joycie, he said – he'd sensed my fear. It'll be OK.

We woke to a fist hammering on the windscreen, and the interior was heating up with the force of the sun, and an old boy was peering in at us as if we'd fallen from the sky. We were actually only five miles from Sabzevar as the crow flew; the old boy let us sit on the back of his cart and we entered the town like a carnival float, a spectacle for the locals. Lucky it was Sabzevar, because there was a one in a million there, a clockmaker who had a passion for foreign vehicles. The fellow greeted us cheerily, sensing a challenge, wiping his hands on his apron. It was going to take a couple of days.

The clutch pedal had stuck to the floor, like a broken jack-in-the-box, Anton said, and the clutch was a goner. The man thought he could remove parts from an old wreck in his yard and transplant them. There were many involved conversations with serious faces, calculating the chances of survival as if it was surgery. Never any certainty, and we felt on edge, nervous of the outcome.

The Magic Bus had moved on ahead of us after we stopped in Tehran, and it was a relief to be in a town with no tourist hostel, no freaks, no talk of the overland, simply to be just the three of us again. To have the boys to myself again! Foreigners rarely stopped in the town, we were as good as a travelling circus. I tried to josh along with the kids who tapped us on the shoulders and ran away hooting and pinched our snacks. We sat among the flies, the hours were stacking up and it became another night. Little girls ran up to look at us and scarpered. The transplant wasn't successful on the first attempt. There was no chance of bumping into someone, there was no one for Freddie to seduce, no hitchhikers, no drug peddlers or groupies. Anton walked off on the second afternoon, touring the town's paltry sights, and Fred and I sat on the back of the van with the back door open, dangling our legs over the bumper.

What are you going to do when you get back to England, Jay-Jay? You should come to stay in Gloucestershire, on the farm. Have a swim in the lake. Did he mean it? Fred was loose with his invitations, but he mentioned it more than once. And perhaps I saw myself then for the first time, returning with the boys to England. Fred pottering down to the local branch line station to collect me in his convertible, insisting on carrying my bags, driving me back through the gates and up the sweeping driveway, waving to Anton, who'd be standing under the immense Palladian portico, waiting impatiently for our return.

I'm going to make my own way, I said. I've got to make my own way too, he replied. For me, it's only this – and he touched the guitar. My great love. He laughed at himself, hesitantly, and I saw the insecurity lurking under the handsome face. I reckon I could have a go at it, you know? I need to find the right guys to play with, just got to get the sound right. A couple of times he'd played with up-and-coming bands at Eel Pie Island, one of the groups was seriously going places. They had wanted him on bass, there was talk of supporting a band that had once supported the Rolling Stones. At Eel Pie, Fred had seen everyone, Joe Cocker, The Who; he'd shared a joint with Syd Barrett of Pink Floyd.

I didn't like to ask what went wrong with the band. Anton had already hinted it was something to do with women, this was before Felicity, possibly the frontman's girlfriend. It takes a lot of self-belief to do that, to stick with your art, I said. I realised that calling it art was pretentious, that I was taking on some of the hippie lingo, calling things art. Clive would have taken the mick. Fred didn't think it was the wrong word, though; he smiled like I'd finally got to the heart of things. I didn't challenge him or try and offer alternatives. Well, there's no choice in it for me, said Fred. That's my destiny. What's your destiny, Joycie? No man waiting for you? I shook my head, didn't go into details, Fred was happy enough with that.

In a nutshell, if I could have articulated it, I'd have said England was my destiny. Because by that point – although I liked those landscapes and those wild places that we drove through, don't get me wrong – a realisation was growing in me, more and more, about the sheer beauty of the English countryside. What place in the world can rival the rugged coastline of Devon? Or the lush green of the Lake District? Is anywhere on the planet in the same class? I saw, in short, that there was still plenty I wanted to return to. That I had an English future. There's no finer nation in the world, I can promise you that – and I have seen a lot of countries.

We left Sabzevar the following morning, the new clutch was a hit and Vera had a new lease of life. Everyone praised that clockmaker from Sabzevar, a saint who performed a miracle for us, Anton nicknamed him Imam Reza, although today I only see his overalls and remember the sound of his whistle as he worked under the chassis of the van. We were in Mashad by that evening.

By now the landscape was becoming stonier, drier. There was a constant sense of upwards inclination, and long, barren stretches where it seemed unlikely anything could thrive or bloom. Anton was so happy during those days, which I found a little baffling, to be honest, given the unpromising landscape. When you compared it to the English fields we'd left behind, it looked so brown, so unforgiving. I've fallen in love with this country! he would say to me, as if he'd found a great lover that he'd been rolling around with all night in bliss.

I've fallen in love with this country. What's that all about? How can you fall in love with rocks and earth and arbitrary borders drawn by men in plus fours and monocles? You can't love all the people in a country, all the shits and swindlers and murderers. No country looks the same from end to end. I can tell you that after all the ways my bum got busted on that journey. Falling in love with a country sounded to me like falling in love with the moon. And we had all done that already, in front of our black-and-white television sets. Falling in love with a country? No, that was a way of saying something else, that you didn't love your own country, or wanted to be loved by people from another country. Anton wanted to be accepted and welcomed by them like a brother, and wanted to be able to fit in without standing out. That's what I thought about Anton's pretentions, if I'm honest, I didn't get them at all. One-way-traffic love. I was pretty sure that the folks of Iran hadn't fallen in love with him. Delusional, really.

There was one Iranian who loved Anton back, though, so maybe I was wrong to rush to such judgements after all. We'd stopped for a while – it was October by then – and Anton decided to employ a tutor for a couple of hours a day, a deadly serious young man who was studying languages at Mashad Technical University. His name was Sameer. They sat together in the courtyard of the mosque opposite the hotel, under the shade of the mulberry tree, and Anton spread out his notecards. The first day he complained, Sameer isn't teaching me anything colloquial. There were no textbooks available, so they were translating newspaper articles and formal pieces of poetry

which Sameer brought on thin pieces of cyclostyled paper.
Sameer ran a tight ship, and after a few days I could hear
them speaking in Farsi, slowly enunciating each word,
before breaking into English.

Anton was sometimes mistaken for a local now, with
his neat black beard, especially once he started wearing a
stone-coloured shalwar and topi from the local market. As
soon as he opened his mouth, though, he was taken for a
ride like any of us. Even his movements were changing; he
was walking with a certain stride, holding his hand against
his breast in greeting.

And when I heard him working out some tricky piece
of syntax with Sameer, or smiling at a joke which didn't
translate well about honey melons or pigeons, I felt, to
be honest, a little panicked. Anton was taking off into a
future from which I would be excluded, that I would never
be able to join. I don't know if you know that feeling?
The glance of a place on the horizon that you know you'll
never reach. They recited couplets, long intricate pieces of
Persian poetry which Anton tried to explain to me. And
in return Sameer asked Anton his views on books, he was
especially taken with E.M. Forster, and had brought along
his grubby Penguin classic. At least, it's meant to be a
classic, but between you and me I've never read it to this
day.

One night after dinner, while we played cards, Anton
said, do you ever think, what the hell are we doing here?
Always the easy questions, Anton, said Fred. I mean, why
on earth are we on the overland? What are we *doing* here?
Because we can be. And the charas is the best in the world,
cheap and bountiful. Sameer says the hippies are spoiling

Iran and they will spoil Afghanistan. Well, Sameer can piss off back to his village. I think he picks up ideas from the other university students, I said, trying to mediate between them, shuffling the pack. I didn't like Sameer much, truth be told; I found him too stern in my presence, he never looked me in the eye or spoke to me directly. He came and went on his scooter with its dirty exhaust, and I thought he looked sinister in his black leather jacket worn over his tunic. He says they're bringing in bad habits, spreading poison. Fred pretended he hadn't heard because Fred wasn't a judgemental person, and he didn't like it when others passed judgement on him.

A few days later, on a side road of Mashad, a freckled, bare-chested fellow was waiting by the van when we returned that afternoon, a red cotton bandana around his head. He grinned toothily at us, and Fred said, far out, it's Chandra! Hail, fellow well met – and they shook hands – my eyes were rolling at Anton as you can imagine. Hop in, old fruit.

He'd been skulking around the Ashti restaurant, the little weasel, bumming fags off people, and he'd heard we were in town and made a beeline for Fred. Chandra with his scruffy blonde dreads and bare feet, and always a roll-up in his fingers. He smelled rancid.

I tried not to let Chandra get my goat. But one day he really got to me. He picked up one of the Persian teacups that I'd just purchased – the very ones still on my shelves in this room; I've always liked their fine enamelling, which contrasts with their delicate copper handles – I might have been boasting a little about what a bargain they were, and he said, what do you need all this crap for, Joyce? You think possessions are the answer? Possessions, not people? I was flustered. Please, put that down. Please. Chandra. And he obeyed me, wrapping it back up in the crumpled newspaper, but with a look that said, that's right, Joyce, keep your guard up. And I felt as if he'd seen right through me.

Chandra had asked for a lift onwards to Kabul. That meant he would be with us for days, possibly weeks. That kicked off things between the two of them. Anton tried his best to protest, but he sounded feeble. So the guy's been to India already. It doesn't make him a swami. I thought we were doing this by ourselves, Anton complained. His real name's probably Kevin or something. And then a few days later he said, Sameer says we shouldn't take Chandra, perhaps as a way of avoiding saying the words himself. He says he's not a good man. He's asking why we are letting him tag along. And why should we care what Sameer thinks? Fred replied. Anton was pained. He was somehow breaking the code of the road; if you had space and someone needed the lift, you took them. It wasn't cool to deny people or cut them loose. Fred won, naturally. Soon Chandra was back with us in the Landy again. I was furiously silent, though Fred didn't seem to notice.

On the morning of our departure we picked Chandra up first from his shabby little hostel, and then we went to Sameer's college, a large, angular building in the suburbs, where Sameer was on his way to class. He embraced Anton and the two of them stood talking, clasping each other's hands, for quite some minutes while the van stood with the engine running. Fred beeped the horn. Sameer gave Anton a dictionary as a leaving gift. And he had brought things for us in a paper bag. Good-quality oranges, the best we'd had for weeks, and a honeydew melon, and some fresh bread that his mother had baked. Sameer shook Fred's hand through the window and smiled a broad smile at me for the first and last time as we revved out of the town. Chandra was asleep, breathing noisily, in the back. Anton was extremely quiet on that stretch of the journey, I noted. And afterwards, he was very particular about that dictionary, and how it had to be wrapped in a special cloth and stored in pride of place in the van.

PART 4

CHICKEN STREET

11

On the way out of Mashad I asked Anton about the vast drums brooding on the horizon. Oil, he said, shipped out east for the Afghans, and sure enough along the road we overtook oil tankers moving eastwards, as well as the usual pickups and flatbeds bulging with fruit and chickens. Afghanistan. Nobody can go there nowadays, can they? When I told my great-niece that I had been, her jaw dropped. She recognised the name from one of her fighting games, and must have pictured me like one of those dusty overloaded soldiers all bundled up tightly in desert camouflage and strapped with guns. Dropped off by an aircraft carrier in a cloud storm, or circling villages in a chopper. It was nothing like that. There was a dried-out no man's land between Iran and Afghanistan and for a while we didn't know which country we were in. It was silent the day I walked into Afghanistan. We just drove across the border.

And we were desperate to get there. Fred wanted to score the famous Afghan black, he had barely been able to smoke anything since Turkey, and Anton wanted to see Herat. I just longed for the border, another threshold, something between a world we believed we had started to understand and another one which opened up before us. The borders became like punctuation marks. One of the only markers that we still had to cling to, to structure our world.

At the border post, a gaggle of foreigners lounged around, in a confused line, complaining about the difficulties of changing money. A compulsory medical inspection followed, and the boys stripped to their trousers while a doctor placed a stethoscope on their chests, listening for the whispers of TB. I could see then, side by side, how thin Fred had got, next to Anton, that blush on his upper arms where his tan met white skin. The doctor asked us where we had been, what we'd been eating, if we were sanitising our water. They're worried about cholera, Anton said. And for a moment I felt nervous in case Fred really was sick, in case the doctor had a special insight into the weakness of his cells, some hidden illness lurking there. His mother died young, after all. But then Fred was prancing like a colt, and out of the door. The doctor took longer with Chandra and his foggy lungs. I was pulled aside behind a blue fabric screen, where a woman sat with a stern expression and a headscarf in military colours. She took my temperature with an ancient thermometer and tapped it as the liquid mercury rose in the glass. Then she stamped a card which was pinned into my passport and waved me through. Outside, a painted white log acted as the gateway to Afghanistan, which a young soldier rolled backwards and forwards to let vehicles pass.

The only fact that everyone knew about Afghanistan was that it was unconquerable. The tribesmen saw off invaders. They had things just the way they liked it. It wasn't that the place was stuck in time, or medieval, or any of that bullshit that people come out with. It was their land, and if they wanted better irrigation or wells or clinics or whatever then they'd arrange for it, and some tribal leader would invite in some Yanks from the peace corps or get some injection of cash from a foreign donor. That's why the travellers liked it there; freedom was the priority.

I gazed out of the window as the country took on a shape of its own. Chandra was sleeping flat-out on the back seats, *quelle surprise*. The land itself and the people had kind of merged into each other. Poppies grew in every field along the roadsides. Men beating out the base of a vast copper-bottomed pot, sitting on charpoys, sharing a pipe, china tea sets printed with roses. And then as we entered Herat, carcasses hung on hooks, flies thick as curtains, too dense to swat away. Men sharing a plate of tiny sweet grapes, the smell of leather tanning and vats of coloured dye. The dominant notes of beige and brown and ochre.

We'd hooked back up with Harjit's Magic Bus and it rolled on in front of us, trundling at the speed of an old banger, rocking with the sway of an elephant. From the driving seat I saw it for many, many hours, the rear of that bus, going on and on, always two lengths in front of me. Once, the Irish guys on the back seat, Enda and Brian, swept aside the back curtain and blew kisses at me. One of them put his mouth on the glass, making a fish face, like a school kid on a trip, then the curtain fell across again and there was nothing, just the dim lights of the interior, and the rear brake lights which flashed red on-off as the bus took bends and ascents. And the dust that came up behind the wheels, the dust which billowed on and on. It was lonely looking at the back of that bus, not knowing what people were doing inside, our own little van riding in the slipstream. Once, the horn blasted out of the blue, making me start and brake, and I never knew if it was a mistake, a slip of the hand, or if Harjit had thought he saw something coming towards us on the single lane, mistaking a shadow for something solid.

We offloaded the next evening in Herat, sweating heavily; the temperature had risen several notches. The men who helped with the bags were courteous, in thick padded jackets despite the heat, and our own men seemed lacking by comparison.

Dope was abundant in Afghanistan. The potheads had been paranoid in Turkey and Iran, keeping their smoking discreet. Now it was an all-out free-for-all. Fred was a kid in a sweetshop, or a bull in a china shop, whichever way you preferred to look at it. The minute we reached Herat, he scored, and then scored again. The guys who sold the hashish made it too easy; they waited for the traffic coming in along the road from the border and they were ready for us, followed us to the little rooms on the back of the bazaar that we'd been directed to. They've got the measure of you, Anton said. Tea appeared, and a huddle of faces, and Fred was shaking hands within the hour. It cuts like a knife through butter, Fred said, wondrous, holding a black patty, a fistful in his hands and lifting it up to Chandra. They talked about the charas as if it was fine wine, inhaling the aroma, examining the texture, connoisseurs. And the young men around the bazaar saw them coming from a mile off. We decided to spend at least a week in Herat, and perhaps that was the mistake.

As I've mentioned, I didn't mind the occasional inhalation back then. But it just didn't do much for me. Hashish made me spaced out, and I needed to be alert. I needed to stay *en garde*. I had no desire whatsoever to fuse with the rest of the universe. I liked a cold beer, but that was hard to come by on those parts of the road, fearsomely expensive in others. You'd suit speed, Fred said one day, as if that was the answer to my deficiencies. For the most part, I just stayed clean and clear-eyed.

The younger Fred had been scared of drugs, he told me much later; drugs meant medicine, long days of doctors with bags and hushed voices, coming and going from his mother's room. A room with sheer white curtains which, in his mind, merged with the hospital room in which she eventually died. He hadn't touched any substances at school, although they had been around at the back of playing fields, traded with boys who had given up on the hope of being prefects or sports captains. He had feared, he told me, doing something wild to his mind. I mean, the mind is capable enough of all kinds of craziness, isn't it? But then I realised, he said, people do so much crazy stuff anyway. Sometimes the most straight people. They can be the worst. They're the ones who love guns and do all that violent shit.

Then, after school, when they were released from their dormitories and the grand house, to live alone in London, there had been parties most nights, in one house or another. He'd tried a few things, lines of coke, mostly big stonking spliffs, as he called them, inhaled on balconies and terraces in Notting Hill and in dank basements in Hammersmith hung with ying yang curtains, and in royal parks on summer days, the sun burning through their eyelids.

All a bit amateur. Not like this, this is the real deal. The real fucking deal, he said. It wasn't good to take it all too far. Cautionary tales swirled around. There was talk of the Europeans who got lost and never came back. A French woman called Suki, living in a cave in the Hindu Kush, married to a tribesman, and her kids were feral; they'd never been to school, didn't know how to read or write. She made beads into jewellery and the kids walked the sides of city roads, selling their trinkets to rich people in Kabul when they pulled up at the traffic lights.

Some of the guys thought I was too straight, most didn't notice or thought I was already stoned. So I watched them all from the sidelines as they went into their circles of giggles or, more usually, their slow, lumbering talk. The same things came round again, free association, topics thrown into the ring and bounced around, the waves of hilarity. The brooding, and always someone horizontal, staring up to the sky. Fred was rolling up before breakfast within days.

Freddie's smoking a lot, isn't he? Anton asked, as if I hadn't already noticed. We're the squares, Anton. Everyone's at it. He looked worried; Anton had known Fred since they were in short trousers. He didn't let me forget that. He's overdoing it. Some of that stuff is strong out here. I had noticed. When is it a problem? When he can no longer drive? I said and it came out of my mouth as a question.

This isn't the place to get into a debate about who was responsible for what went wrong on that journey. Young people have a puritanical streak these days, and they don't understand the way people used substances back then. I'd seen people doing a lot by this point, I wasn't naïve: pills swigged with hooch, mushrooms of all varieties, a lot of brightly coloured pills, the uppers and the downers, to perk you up or help you sleep. Everyone was on something. What Fred chose to get up to was his business, as far as I was concerned. But when he took up smoking all day with Chandra in a little den, that's when warning bells started to ring.

Anton said, have you tried having a conversation with him recently, it's like he's swimming through treacle. Do you think we should try and get him away from that dope? He looked worried. And I said something like, if he's going to be that stupid, he can make his own bed and lie in it. That was the view in those days, fundamentally, it was your life to get right, or screw up, and everyone had to make their choices. You make your own reality, and then you live with the consequences. I still buy into some of those ideas to this day, to be frank.

I didn't think the boys *really* had to worry about anything. Tell me, what did they have to fret about compared to me? I knew I'd have to start my life from scratch once I got home. For Anton the trip was a cul-de-sac on the way back to ordinary life. He had a lot of cards to play back in London: fancy education, qualifications, he knew all the right people. He was never going to struggle to get a job. Even lower stakes for Fred, he was ordained to lord it over a hundred acres of Gloucestershire. Yes, Fred's burial plot had been allocated on the day he was born; he would return to the soil of that parish churchyard, I was sure of that. His coffin would be lowered into his family land. I never would have guessed how wrong I could be.

Fred must have lived off raisins and bread the whole time we were in Herat. I can't say I liked the meat much in Afghanistan – mutton in stringy stews, grease on the surface, that was what people ate in those parts. Fred had been a fusspot ever since he'd started insisting – somewhere in western Turkey – that as well as no meat, no gravy and no vegetables if they'd been cooked in animal juices would pass his mouth. He was determined. Way too violent, too bloody, he had said. We saw how they suspended goat meat down little lanes, and how knives were sharpened on foot-powered wheels. Hulks of meat carcass, thick with flies. In the afternoon, we insisted Fred come round the bazaar with us, under the shadow of the citadel, looking for fruit which wasn't bruised or wormy. So you're ruling out restaurants and solid meals and basic nutrition? Anton complained. You do know this is the worst trip in the world on which to decide to become a vegetarian? I guess Chandra was probably a vegetarian too, it would have fit, but looking back I don't remember him eating much at all… or doing much at all.

While Anton and I were off seeing the Jama Masjid and the shrine at Gazur Gah and going to the market and the post office, taking horse-drawn tongas out into the world, Fred and Chandra made a dank little den of that room at the back of the bazaar. The way that Freddie rolled up had changed, his fingers now working more quickly, expertly, and with little ceremony. His nails were always black, especially under the thumbnail where he'd broken off charas and rolled it into the tiny pieces to be dotted in the tobacco. And when he breathed in, it was deep into the furthest portion of his lungs so that the smoke billowed all around his head, his chest, his face, his mouth, encircling and mystifying him further as he made audible exhalations.

The post restante in Herat was a cardboard box in the care of a postmaster in a dirty white turban. After we'd rifled through and pulled out anything addressed to us – there was just one letter for Anton and nothing for me – the postmaster asked us if we wanted tea, and sent a barefoot boy about seven years old running to bring chai in patterned glasses. We sat with him a while, and he started speaking in Farsi with Anton, so they were switching in and out of languages, and I could only pick up part of the conversation which was about the shrine of a poet. Then the old postmaster offered to sell us hashish, and Anton looked exasperated, and said – perhaps to himself, or to me – people in this place are obsessed. That's what they think all the travellers want.

All the while Anton had been holding the thick envelope in his hand, turning it over absent-mindedly in his fingers, a green ink-stamp on it, smudgy, which read SOAS. The result of his university application. Are you going to open it? He looked unsure of himself, and pushed his glasses up his nose. Anton was the boff, there never seemed to be any doubt about it; when he opened the letter, and he unfolded it with care, there was the news that he had been hoping for. A typed sheet on letterhead informing him that he was admitted to the bachelors' degree in Farsi starting in September at the School of Oriental and African Studies, University of London. He had been awarded an undergraduate scholarship for his first year, and I remember the exact words, 'in recognition of his potential'. I'm not sure I ever saw Anton as happy as that day. He explained to the postmaster the contents of the letter and the old man clinked his tea glass with him and sent the child running off again for sweets, which came back little golden globes, sticky as honey.

Anton wanted to share his good news with Fred, and once we returned to the guest house he stood there at the doorway with his university letter in his hand. Fred had heard him, though he hadn't heard him; he was nodding and agreeing and absent, so that even when he said, congratulations, mate, his heart wasn't in it. He was completely focused on teaching a small Afghan boy the guitar. The instrument was way too big for the kid so Fred had to sort of prop it up with his knee to balance it, and he was reaching over the boy's shoulders, showing him how to place his fingers on the fret. The little boy was wearing a baggy tunic which fell to his knees, and he had dust on his face and on his feet, and he looked as if his life depended on the mastery of that chord. Fred was patient with the lad, and, admittedly, he taught him lovely little tunes all week. But shouldn't Fred have paid more attention to Anton's success? Fred was always giving his love away to complete strangers, foreigners even, who didn't deserve his care as much as we did. It was frustrating for Anton – I could see that.

The weight had fallen off Fred, seeing him there from the doorway from a distance. He was wearing thin pyjama trousers and a little waistcoat with a ribbon trim. He had his hair drawn back into a ponytail with a rubber band and a sticking plaster over one earlobe; he'd found some local barber where they did piercings with a hot needle. I reminded him to bathe it with disinfectant and make sure it healed up to avoid infection. I guess we were all changing, maybe it was just harder to see it on yourself. Fred was a peacock, a smell coming off him too not what you'd expect, not weed and sandalwood joss sticks, the way Chandra smelled, though there was probably a top note of that too; rather some sort of camphor, a little pot of balm that he rubbed into his temples and his lips. Not unpleasant, medicinal.

Chandra was the one who started Fred on mescaline, and on acid. There was a bit more to Chandra as it turned out, he'd read a lot, could talk about experiments with LSD at Berkeley in California, about taking voyages to new realms of consciousness, about the ways that a personality could be rewired through the experience of tripping, that consciousness could be expanded if people could act without fear. He said it was proven, without doubt, scientifically – some prisoners given psychedelics in America were swearing off crime. Chandra, it became apparent, was a lot more coherent than I'd given him credit for. If, through some trick of nature, the gates of an individual's subconsciousness were to spring open, without warning, Chandra declared, the unprepared mind would be overwhelmed and crushed. So the gates of the subconscious had been guarded, hidden behind a veil of mysteries and symbols. Now we had the keys. I could believe that, I just wondered if Fred was ready. Giving Fred the keys didn't seem like such a bright idea. A trip just reflects what's going on inside your subconscious, Chandra said. He could be chatty for a hippie. Some of the sadhus, they are so enlightened, acid has no effect on them at all; they're immune to it, they're already on another plane.

Well, if that was the case, then Fred, naturally, was fairly well done for. No one had done less thinking about his subconscious than Fred. He hadn't even peeked under the bonnet, and now there he was dissolving tabs under his tongue and taking off into other dimensions.

Chandra said it wasn't my business, that Fred had to work it out for himself. And that he understood that his awareness could expand beyond ego, self, family, beyond notions of space and time, beyond the differences which usually separate people from each other and from the world around them.

That was the time things really started cracking up.

12

We started early the next morning, wanted to drive ahead of the heat. The road threading south from Herat to Kandahar was paved, Russian-built, cutting a line through the desert, so the start was strong. We stocked up with the Russian petrol for sale along the roadside, and Anton said we might even have a swim at a hotel on the way, though when we reached the Continental it was derelict, a large concrete hotel with an empty swimming pool, many millions of wasted roubles. Yanks and Russians had been competing over that place, trying to develop Afghanistan – what on earth was the point? Those folks had decided they didn't want swimming pools.

As we wound down the valley, the hills rose up on either side and took on new shapes, and Anton became more excited, pulling out his camera from the leather case, and the sensation of climbing down took on a queasy sensation as if the back of the van might flip over the front. The road deteriorated.

It was like a film, the pace of it, the colour of it, as if

shot on a Super 8 for our own enjoyment. Granular, beige
reams of life unspooling before us, as if it could all be re-
spooled, wound up, forgotten. As if the people we saw,
motionless or slow – women walking with hips swaying
under the weight of jars of water, children in rags – were
made of a different matter, put there with their head
baskets and their bicycles loaded with bundles by an artist.

That night the stars on those plains, those dark hostile
horizons, were incredible. Extravagant. Wasted on us. We
were somewhere on a long road, I wish I remember now
where, it curved up into the mountains, and down onto
the plains below, ancient abandoned forts, looming, and
the place names running into each other, and we tended
to forget them once we'd gone past them, everyone fixing
on the next destination, place names like an incantation,
only to be passed, before taking up another spell-name,
and thinking of the hours until the bus would stop again.

On some of those long stretches, Fred started ranting
a little. Maybe it was the substances, or maybe he'd been
storing things up inside himself for a long time. He wasn't
going to take a penny from his father anymore, that was
the first thing he said. Not just once, but again, loudly,
in the car, in cafés, to me, to Anton direct. Not a penny.
Going to make it on my own. I'll believe it when I see
it, said Anton, accelerating slightly, and making the van
clunk uncomfortably over a hump in the road.

And then there were some long lectures about wasting
time on history, how looking into the past was a waste of
time. Fred didn't have a lot of factual knowledge, despite
the expensive education; what he did know was instinctive,
tricksy, picked up on the road. He had a way of spinning

arguments and making Anton feel stupid. He took his facts and history books and made light of them. As if logic was an old, Victorian way of looking at the world, and there were hidden meanings that you'd never get out of books, however hard you tried. Anton, we all know you're clever, Fred said, but is it good for much? Out here in the world? Anton tried to formulate an answer, but he didn't really have one. Fred had got to him alright.

Fred had old ghosts to reckon with. His acid trips turned into boxing matches, dramas, the final acts of tragedies. Fred had some inner impulse, always, to go further, to push himself over some limit, the line which we all knew was too dangerous to cross.

On the second day of driving, about two hours outside Kandahar, we took a break at a roadside stall, fly-blown interior, with wooden benches and hard bread and watery tea. We'd left Chandra asleep in the van. Anton said he was going to fill up the tank with the jerry can and Fred and I fumbled with coins, dealt with the bill.

When Fred and I came out of the tea shack, Anton was with two people I didn't recognise, standing by a cream Citroen. They looked sharp-edged against the horizon. One of them was a woman in butterfly sunglasses, another a tall man in a safari suit. Look who we ran into, Fred! Anton was scowling, I knew him well enough by now. Felicity!

It took me a moment to digest this information, to square the beautiful woman in front of us, standing against the door of a Citroen, with the woman who had broken Fred's heart. I couldn't make sense of how we had bumped into them. It seemed so unlikely given the remoteness of the place, though the trail was like that – there were only so many places people stopped, only so many points on the map. How on earth could they be here on the road to Kandahar in that dinky little car?

She had a gap between her front teeth which was peculiarly attractive and an unusually upright posture, young muscles trained in ballet or horse riding. She was wearing tight jeans with a decorated Pakistani blouse, which looked daring and unlike any outfit I'd seen on the road. Her small, peachy bottom was tucked in snug. She was a match for Fred alright.

They kissed on both cheeks in the French style. Fred had a bemused expression on his face. He fiddled with his tobacco pouch, rolling a small cigarette, and licked the paper for her with the edge of his tongue before handing it over. He didn't seem unduly disturbed to see his ex. Freddie, I would not have recognised you. She held the cigarette he had rolled between her fingers. You look well, he said. Marriage suits me. Laurent and I got married. Didn't you hear? She had a simple gold band on her finger. She didn't look a day over twenty-one. We didn't make a fuss. Registry office in Kensington, though his family want the whole Catholic shebang once we get back. We're going to live in Paris. She looked defiantly at Fred. We're just up from Islamabad. We've been in Pakistan for a while. Laurent is exporting rugs. Checking out the new garment factory. We're flying out next week. I winced – poor Fred! – and I was amazed that he didn't seem more fussed by this turn of events.

Laurent was a little stoned and looked like a catalogue model. He was impeccably dressed in white linen, completely white, not a speck on it; miraculous in the circumstances. I could scarcely believe that they'd arrived in this same place without enduring the same journey as us, without suffering along thousands of miles of potholes and pissing in holes in the ground. None of it seemed fair. Felicity was still doing all the talking and as she spoke, she swept a scarf over her head in the Pakistani style, a light pink gauze.

Laurent's family firm were expanding their production, Felicity explained. A new range of what she called haberdashery, made in Pakistan, and there was a team developing the factory in Islamabad. She thought that Islamabad was dull, everything too recently built and sterile in the new city, and she'd persuaded Laurent to take a week in the Afghan hills, a jaunt, and wasn't it just such a surprise, darlings, to run into us.

Naturally they were going to Kandahar too. We followed their car all the way. I guessed it must have been torture for Fred to sit up there behind the wheel, watching his lover's head bob along in front in that little car, with the impeccable Laurent beside her. When we reached Kandahar, the mountains were turning different shades of lilac.

That evening a ridiculous comedy of errors ensued – it wouldn't have happened if the planning had been down to me. Three guest houses were full to the rafters and turned us away, and then we lost Chandra for about half an hour. Felicity and her beau stood by their Citroen, smoking calmly, and she said – I don't know why you're making such a fuss, just come and stay with us. It's no trouble. We'd love to have you. Anton grimaced. He tried to make some excuses. Fred said, Flick, you are a brick! And laughed at his own rhyme. You've got space for these two as well? I heard him whisper, as he gestured towards me and Chandra as if we were hangers-on, and I have to say I was a little affronted by that.

On the other hand, I was excited about spending more time with Felicity. I wanted to be in her orbit. I thought she might confide in me, and explain what had happened between them; that she'd be pleased to see another woman from England who would have so much in common with her. I felt that her radiance could somehow be refracted; her light might bounce back onto me, and then we could bond.

The stars were breaking out as we approached. It was a very fine house, hewn out of an old fortress, with wooden shutters and a polished floor and a roof terrace which she led us to, with views of the old citadel on one side, and, on the other, the mudbrick fortifications and the minarets of the city like candles in the distance. She had taken possession of the house, and somehow there were waiters and cooks to wait on us, they called her madam, and brought out dishes in clay pots. The house wasn't very practical, she said, very dusty, there were plenty of rooms, though. It seemed like a prolongation of pain. I felt sorry for Fred and gave him a sympathetic look.

There were about ten of us around the table on the rooftop, some Americans from USAID who Felicity had also gathered up along the way, and a Swiss man who was attempting the overland by bicycle, legs like rope. Chandra nodded and beamed beatific smiles and fortunately didn't say much. Bread was passed around in circles, we all shared the dishes. Felicity looked very much at ease, even though she was far too manicured to be among us.

So what are you running away from? she said to me, and I noticed how expertly she scooped up her meat and rice with the bread, as if she was completely composed in every country and every culture. She was still wearing her flimsy top, and at close quarters I could examine how beautifully elaborate the stitching was, the tiny little intricate flowers and beads. I saw myself through her eyes. It was like meeting royalty.

Bad men, I said, hoping to try and forge some sisterly solidarity with her. I'd heard other women on the trail say similar phrases, and I was starting to feel that there was some truth in it. Oh, Christ. Are you a feminist? She rolled her eyes as if I'd just admitted to being a communist. Men aren't all bad, are they? And she glanced over at Freddie with unconcealed admiration. How's he been? Fred has been a bit freaky, I said. I wanted her to be intrigued, maybe to acknowledge what we'd put up with, all that we'd done for Fred, all that she had, in fact, caused. I wanted to give her the hint – that Fred talked to me about intimate things, about screwing her, in fact. He's wild, Freddie, off the wall. She said, smugly, he wrote to me. We arranged this. You didn't think it was a coincidence that we ran into you, did you? I had to see him. I had to break the news of our marriage to him in person.

I wanted to ask her why she'd cast off Freddie, how she could leave him in ruination then return to rub salt into the wound, but she'd already glanced away. I was an irrelevance to her. Too ordinary, too plain. Just someone who'd answered an advertisement in a newspaper. She barely spoke to me after that. Her body was skewed towards Fred. Laurent seemed to have trouble following the conversation and occasionally she translated for him into perfect French, then kissed him ostentatiously. Anton was caught up with the Swiss cyclist, who had produced maps.

When I look back now, I think that Felicity wasn't all that special. Don't get me wrong – she was beautiful, no doubt about it. But I have seen many beautiful women in my time, and I realise now that she was putting on a sort of show, but at the time I was rather impressed with her, as Fred had been. I thought she, in the parlance of the times, 'had it all', and I went up to bed rather despondent that she hadn't recognised that I could be a kindred spirit.

My room was lovely, in a ghostly way. There was an old wooden bed with turned posts, which creaked and the mattress gave out clouds of dust when I hit it. I couldn't sleep. I felt that maybe Fred would want some company. I wanted to commiserate with him. Perhaps he would share the real story behind his break-up with Felicity and then we might feel closer. I had some undeveloped idea that I might try and heal his pain.

Moonlight was pouring through the diamonds in the lattice of the window. I lay on the bed, turning this way and that, and decided to seek him out. His room was across the corridor. It was about midnight, and Fred was always the last to sleep. A crack of candlelight flickered from under the door and muffled sounds came from within.

I suppose I might have knocked, though we didn't always knock in those days, or I may have just pushed the door open a tiny crack in case he was asleep, and I didn't want to wake him. It was confusing to see, until I understood what it was, a tangle of bodies on the floor, a mess of pale sheets, and then white and round, Fred's arse in the air, humping vigorously. And underneath, beautiful small white breasts, bouncing. I didn't understand, nearly fled, but something pulled me back to watch a little more, and then I understood that the breasts and the body were Felicity's and it was Felicity's voice I could hear, whispering to Fred, encouraging him, gripping his arse with an intensity that looked violent, possibly dangerous.

Fred wasn't so self-centred after all. He was down on his knees, pushing her legs apart. The sound of her cries terrified me – she was ready to tip over so quickly, so full of erotic charge and so alive with the feeling of him, so unconscious – how was it possible to turn off the brain to such an extent, to leave yourself so naked and vulnerable? I was disgusted, and fascinated. And jealous? Perhaps, though, I thought, what a fool, you need to watch your back, you're putting yourself at risk, girl, spreading yourself out like that. I wanted to pull her away and make sure she was out of harm's way.

I closed the door and ran back to my room. The next morning Felicity and Laurent were gone.

The following day Freddie was glum in the car, obstinate, wouldn't help Anton when the van needed jacking up and a tyre changing. Hardly took his turn with filling up the jerry cans with water, and when he did help, did it reluctantly, like a boy ordered to do things by his parents. Even Chandra was more use that day. She'd done a number on him.

Somehow it didn't make sense either, that Felicity

could cause him such pain. He could have had any other woman on the road, and he knew it. He was surrounded by groupies, and his unfaithful heart was too young for pinning down. I felt that Fred knew that too. I came to think that Felicity was a muse for Fred, that he needed to be morose and have a woman to feel down about, because that would help his music along. I thought he was pining for her because he realised he'd let her go, and she was the source of his genius. Without her he felt he was nothing.

I asked Anton while we loaded the van in Kandahar and he told me as he lifted the bedrolls and stuffed them into the rear, jammed between boxes, in any spare space. Oh no, it was the other way round, he assured me. Felicity would have married Fred, no doubt about it. He was the one who ran away, took off on this trip. He was the one not ready for settling down. She has babies in her sights, and she liked the look of the pile. The earl was onside. She seems fey, though she's a loyal heart. She loved Freddie, she was quite obsessed with him. So what went wrong? I handed him another stack of bedding. Fred's fickle, you know that. He gets carried away. He told her he didn't believe in marriage. It was bad timing, he was too young, much more he wanted to do. The music came first. And then, when she pulled the plug, he couldn't handle the break-up. Silly old Fred.

I rolled up some blankets and cushions and wedged them in the gaps between the bedrolls. I had a break-up too, I blurted. Oh, great, we're the lonely hearts club band. Welcome to the show.

13

We navigated endless brown waves of desert, barren hills of rock and sand. I saw a lone boy selling Cokes from a cool box in the desert. Nights by candlelight when the electricity flickered off. Thick black layers of flies in the toilets. There was grit under my eyelashes, and a rim of salty black dirt around my neck. We waited for tough men herding dried-out camels across the road, beating them on with sticks. Heads wound with turbans. Men on their haunches. We sucked slices of watermelon. Dry land, the colour of hard bread. Quick, loud sounds punctured the air; the burst of a drum, or playful rifle fire.

My constitution stayed solid, even though others got knocked out by dysentery and the whole litany of overland woes. I found I was made of stronger metal. Everyone showed that trip on their body, a mosquito bite gone rancid or a motorbike exhaust that singed the ankle we called an Enfield tattoo. I toughed it out. That's something you have to understand about me. Even today I can count on one hand the times I have been in hospital.

You have a solid constitution, Joyce, Chandra said in a mocking tone.

Anton succumbed to all sorts of petty itches and bites, and by the time we were halfway across Afghanistan I felt he was wearying. He would never admit it. Perhaps, I think now, he might have preferred to have viewed all the old sights in books. Would he have been happier to learn about it in a library and to hold the calligraphed manuscripts in white gloves? He soldiered on with his sighs and his little arch comments and went through the whole rigmarole with Vera day after day, which was hot and mechanical work, seeing her spark plugs right, tanking her up. He was not cut out for manual labour. The old girl was like me – tough as old boots – and the pair of us were determined to get to India in one piece, and I felt a kinship with the van which might sound strange given she was only metal and parts. Fred called her Chitty Chitty Bang Bang and said, imagine she could just fly us up to Nepal, and I almost believed that she could.

Then Vera started going through a rough patch. Just got to pray it's not terminal, said Fred. The battery kept going flat when we least expected it, stalling on uphill inclines and then we would need to get out and push, Fred looping an arm through the window to steer, placing his shoulder hard to the side door, while Anton and I heaved from behind. When the road was steep I feared the van rolling back onto us, crushing our toes under the solid black tyres, and at times we'd be joined by Pathans who appeared at the roadside, called by children, whooping and running, and a team would assemble from nowhere for the big push, clapping or cheering spontaneously when the engine growled back into life.

Anton thought we'd need at least a few days in Kabul with a proper mechanic. The different surgical options were discussed. Chandra never took a view. Just sat dumb while we argued it out. We were placing a lot of faith in Kabul's mechanics. We stopped playing music, worried that the radio would strain the feeble battery. In the silence I could tell that Fred was stressed, he needed a fix. Chandra handed him a pill from time to time. He stopped looking into the back of the van to check on how I was doing, withdrew into himself. On the second day of driving, when the car stopped again as it was getting darker and colder, Fred yelled out, Christ Almighty!, thumping the roof in frustration. I simply won't do it again. He hadn't smiled all day. No choice, mates, said Anton.

Anton was always worried about Fred on those days. He eyed him with suspicion, expected him to trip and fall. Chandra was no help at all. Something for the road, Fred? he said, and he handed Fred a medicine bottle again and Fred, with a sigh of relief, took the contents in one swift move. The car limped into Kabul.

We had made it that far. We'd done almost five thousand miles by that point. And we had less than a thousand to go, onwards to Pakistan and then down into India and the final miles into Nepal. But Kabul didn't feel like a triumphal entry.

This place has seen better days, said Anton, it's gone to seed. Kabul was crammed with modern concrete buildings and full of too many travellers – frankly too many stoned heads – packed into a tiny quarter of the city; there were a lot of nutcases shacked up there. Some of them looked like they would never leave, or couldn't leave, and an area called Chicken Street was overflowing with little shops, with corrugated roofs where the stall owners competed for our attention and called out to us every time we walked past. The stalls sold lapis lazuli, and tiger skins, and furs and sun-faded leather and carpets that nobody could afford and rows of crocodile teeth – I'll admit I did pick up one or two fine little blue gems from those stalls. There were still bargains to be had. One of those lapis I later had set in gold which I like to wear on my ring finger. In fact, it has been mistaken for an engagement ring over the years; I'm looking down on it now on my hand as I write this.

We were staying at the Faloodah House, right off Chicken Street. While checking in, Anton asked for my passport, and I handed it over without thinking. The man at the desk stared at the pages, blinking, making sense of our strange consonants, and then inscribed our names and passport numbers into the foreigners' ledger. When the passports were handed back, as we gathered our bags, Anton flicked through the pages in his curious way. Joycie, why's your passport in a different surname? Your letters are addressed to another name, right? I was jolted into stillness, my mind trying to find a way through; a way to avoid shame. No reason, I said. He looked at me in a way which meant, pull the other one. He was too good at details. Oh, Joyce, come on; I tell you everything. He looked hurt, as if I was keeping a secret from him, which, to be fair, I was.

As we followed the guy up to the first floor, heaving

our backpacks up the stairs, he wouldn't let it drop. That's a different surname. Is that your mother's name or something? I was cornered, unable to find a way to dodge the questions, too tired from the road or slow-witted to imagine a better story than the truth. I leaned against the door of my room. I was married. Excuse me? Anton looked as if I was pulling his leg. I still am married, actually, in technical terms. Well, aren't you the dark horse, Joycie, he said, enjoying the news and my discomfort. Don't tell the others, alright? Who's the lucky fellow? It's not a joke, Anton. Seriously. Well, well, I can't wed them if I want to, and you can't wait to be rid of them. Isn't the world topsy-turvy?, although his face was softening into concern, because maybe he'd seen how I was starting to redden.

Come and have some wine, he said. We had a few bottles left over from Trixie's cellar. There was an understanding that it was preserved for emergency situations. Anton pulled the cork out with a penknife. It was a juggernaut that had taken on momentum, I couldn't stop, I said; I could have handled the humiliation of a broken engagement, even being stood up at the altar, looking down the aisle. I went through with all of it, on a wing and a prayer, ignored the hunch in my gut; the cucumber sandwiches and the throwing of the bouquet, and all those piles of cards and gifts. The staged photographs of happy families. Everything had been planned in the most predictable way.

It sounds odd to young people today, but that was how you left home in my town. There was no prospect of living together. A boyfriend was tolerated for a while, while you lived with your parents, and then at some point you had to grow up and take the plunge. And the men knew it too;

they had to pop the question and provide for you. We all knew the rules of the game.

So the town hall was booked. Mum made the dress, Dad stumped up the cash. I wasn't too fussed about the details – I let my mother take care of them – I wanted to get on with the business of living and doing it in our own bed. Three weeks after the marriage I walked out. It was a mistake, I said to everyone, I made a poor choice. Anton didn't press for details; perhaps they were there on my face.

And now I was stained with the dye, a divorcee forever. Tainted before life had even started, or that was how it had felt. Although, as I recounted the story to Anton up in that room and he poured out more warm wine into an enamel mug, I felt for the very first time that it was only a story, and that the overland was more important in my life than my ill-fated marriage.

Sounds like a total loser to me, said Anton, and I slid down the side of the bedspread into a heap of giggles on the floor. How did you let him know? I got his mother to come over. We fell into laughter again, and I was truly seeing again that dour old bird in her housecoat, with her pressed lips. I recovered my composure and straightened my face. It was serious, no joking matter. Don't tell the others, alright? I want to forget it, to put it behind me. Alright he said, I can tell you, though, I think marriage is servitude and dreary sex. He said the other conventional words that others had said to me at the time – clouds and silver linings and so on – but this was the first time I believed them. And as he did so, he stroked the back of my head, and I sat there on the floor, weeping for my naïve little self who had wanted that fairy tale, had wanted the icing and the cake decorations and the little girls in flounces. He ran a comb through my hair as if I was a small girl, disentangling it, making me better, and I realised that perhaps Anton should have been a doctor like his dad, that his touch could heal. And from that day onwards, he never did tell a soul.

In Kabul, a mechanic did materialise, and we went with him to a car graveyard, where the old shells of blasted-out European cars and vans lay about, every conceivable piece removed or amputated. Fiats without wheels, various vans with all their layers of graffiti, peace signs and the names of the travellers painted on the outside, the running tally of the places they'd been through, the same towns as us – Istanbul, Erzurum, Herat – flags and stickers from those who'd come before us, from Switzerland, Germany, Australia. Every piece of metal fitting, wing mirrors, side doors, had been yanked off, repurposed, sold on. There was even an old London Routemaster, tilting to one side, tomato red, a number 24, the destination read Kathmandu, and it was a sorry sight, the abandonment of that dream. Flowers on the side of the bus, it had become a place that the local street kids hung out and scrambled in and out of the window frames, which had once held glass, and spread themselves out on the rear seats, whistling at us and laughing.

Well, this is sodding useless, said Fred; he was frustrated and snapping at everyone. We're not going to find anything here. The mechanic was looking at a shabby Land Rover, not dissimilar to Vera, a bleached-out blue, as if it might hold answers, crouching down to inspect the front of the bonnet. I didn't like to look at that Land Rover, motionless and faded; it had lost all its pride. It was like a spectre of the future, everything that we feared. On the rear seat was a cigarette packet, empty and crumpled. Crushed by a fist. English, said the mechanic, and then I saw the number plate. English kids who had been this way before us. Why had their journey ended here? I didn't want to ask. Come on, said Anton, let's get the hell out of here.

What's eating Fred? I asked Anton that evening. Ask him, he shrugged, then, look, Fred takes things to heart. Can't you talk with him? I asked. Boys aren't always the best talkers. When Fred's mother died, it was announced in the school chapel service, he told me, and the boys had tried their level best – giving Fred the most popular sweets from their tuck boxes – as if to compensate for the loss of a mother, and never talked about it once. So we let Fred carry on his own little personal mission to get as wrecked as humanly possible, unable to see any other option.

The day I most worried about Fred was the day when when he ate meat. Perhaps ten days after we reached Kabul, sitting in a place near the Faloodah Guest House, he said, I'm going to have the kebab too. Bring another plate, will you? And then he tucked in, as if meat eating was something that he was used to. Erasing the time of discipline, undoing all that careful ordering and menu reading, the evenings of denial. And let's face it, he didn't deny himself much. I need something in it, he announced. Protein or something. Can't harm. Why did he do that? It troubled me. The saddest concession I've ever seen a man make. He knew the game was up somehow, that whatever came next was going to be beyond his control and he was trying to fortify his body against a coming onslaught.

He tended not to trip in front of us, we don't have the right energy, Anton said, sardonic. Fred would go off for a few days, to Bamiyan once, I think, at other times he would be with Chandra and his friends in a guest house that I didn't want to enter, with fringed door hangings and an owner with a five o' clock shadow who dozed by the entrance, on a plastic chair, pretending to be oblivious to what was happening in the upstairs rooms. Fred would go a day or two without being seen, without eating, and then reappear at the café, thirsty as a man come from the desert, and lie there smiling and looking up at the ceiling, while I bought endless bottles of Fanta. Then there was the fire in that place, which could have been so much worse – nobody ever admitted to knocking over that candle but the room was gutted; I guess Fred bought his way out of that mess. The boy was unravelling, cracking up, and we didn't know how to help him, and when I think about it now it's not as if we could have done anything differently, could we? It just sort of spiralled from then on.

Should we have done more? It was a shame to feel Fred slipping from us, our trio pulling at the seams, but Anton was so full of excitement about the prospect of seeing places – the Shamshira mosque and Babur's tomb – and then there were all the hours of stories sitting around low tables in the evenings; and then the Irish boys, Enda and Brian, along with Big Red, the Canadian, turned up. Look what the cat brought in, someone called out as they showed up late at night with their backpacks; those guys, who had been pasty and undesirable, had shed weight, stripped down to their jeans, grown stubble and longer hair; they were barely recognisable. Anton gave them high-fives and Brian wrapped me in a hug.

We were so chuffed to see them and to hear about the sorry tale of the Magic Bus and how they'd jumped ship and waved it off as it U-turned west. The bus had fallen to smithereens, they said, Harjit the driver had been on the edge of a nervous breakdown. Some of the passengers had started to get nasty, thinking about the sixty pounds they'd handed over with the promise of getting to Delhi, and someone had had to give him Valium. Harjit ended up on crutches and was forced to hand over the driving to one of the passengers. As Enda put it, they'd made the call to split off on their own. Since then they'd hitched, biked and stumbled their way across Afghanistan and it had all taken them twice the time they'd budgeted. I wonder what happened to Harjit, and to his sister and her Pakistani snog, and what his mother said when she discovered he'd never even graced the gates of Amritsar, let alone found himself that Punjabi bride.

I learned to play backgammon and wasn't too bad at it. A couple of weeks passed, it was the end of October. And it felt for the first time that I could let Fred out of my sight, and that I could make do without him. I was getting more serious about buying bits and bobs, spending a long time at the markets, hunting out old statuettes and tiny bronze Buddha heads small enough to pocket. Some lovely little things; I have them all here with me now, lined up in a row. There are some objects I regret leaving behind, and sometimes I imagine how the journey would have come to pass if I'd more money with me, or the wherewithal to buy some of the better-quality antiques.

Once we saw these workmen carrying out a large Buddha's head that had been sawn clean off its body. The serene contentment on his sideways face. They hauled the head – it was massive, at least twice the size of a real human head – and carried it horizontally, like old furniture. Dull gold with a thin band around its forehead, encrusted with precious stones, and I could see flecks of vermillion scattered by worshippers, and traces of petals, remnants of offerings, that had stuck to the surface of the face. The hair was carved into tiny, tight tendrils, the eyes firmly closed. A holy head. From a temple. Severed. Anton said it was an assault. But what I wouldn't give to get my hands on that thing now! What a beauty. Worth a fortune. Anton was upset about it, stupidly, I thought – the head had already been chopped off, so it felt ludicrous to stand there blocking their path. I made him stand aside and we watched them trundle up the street, heaving the Buddha round the corner of the narrow lane. That was a miss. And we know nowadays that I was right, and how much better-preserved things like that are in places like the British Museum, which can adjust the humidity in their glass cabinets and can employ the best conservators in the world. I know some people disagree, and say the British should have left things where they found them, but then I remember those Afghans, just flogging off the family silver whenever they got the chance.

A day or two passed when I didn't see Fred at all and

I made the most of it, pushing him to the recesses of my mind. Enda and Brian were fun, free spirits, staying just the right side of sensible. Tales of getting wrecked and run-ins with the local law, all with Brian's enactments and accents. Enda said one night, we've both had it with Dublin, we can't see a fair future. We want out, it's going to get worse before it gets better. He had his heart set on Australia. They tried to be nice about it, although they couldn't hide what they felt about the English. It's not you, it's your army, they said, and I didn't take it personally.

The younger one, Brian, looked at me a certain way, no pains to hide it, sweetly, blushing under his freckles, and I liked to feel his gaze on me when I was studying the counters on the backgammon board, considering my next move. It was the first time I'd entertained a thought like that on the trip, and he was hanging around me one evening and suggested a game, and I even thought, for a moment, about walking back with him to the hostel, and letting him slip an arm around my waist.

That next afternoon, the lad suggested a walk – after I let him beat me – with a grin from Big Red, and I felt myself drawn to him in a way that I hadn't felt for many months, perhaps not towards anyone but Fred, for a very long time. I was contemplating his offer of a rematch. And then came the sound of urgent shouting, an earnest yelling in the street, which turned heads. Immediately I recognised the voice as Anton's, and then a shout of alarm, Joyce!

Joyce, you've got to come, come quickly. It's Fred. A note of panic in his voice which was new, which brought strangers out of the teashop. I ran barefoot into the lane, where Anton stood arms open in the road, his palms facing upwards and a look of despair which I will never forget on his face. Thank God you're here, he said. I couldn't find you, it's Fred, you've got to come. He took off up the lane at a sprint, and I ran after him, leaving everything behind. For a second I wondered if he was dead, and I knew we wouldn't be running so fast if he was dead, and my first feeling was one of pure relief when I saw Fred, every bit alive, standing on a table.

He was on a square near the Faloodah House, in his jeans but his top was off, with all the Afghans sitting around laughing, looking up at him, as he spun round and round. A dervish. He's tripping pretty bad, said a guy with long dreadlocks. What's he dropped? I asked. Acid. Chandra was there with a look of bemused nonchalance on his freckled face. A couple of the stoned freaks around us looked up from their joints, mildly interested. A girl reading a book said, wild, but in a deadpan voice. The etiquette was not to be shocked. It's going to be a few days, said an older guy with a moustache and a worn face, sipping tea. His face said he knew the trail, he had done this route the hard way many times. Give him time.

Fred, it's me, Joyce, I said, reaching up my arms. I tried to hold his hands and look him in the eye, but they were dancing too. He was as far away as at the end of a trunk call; he was there and not there, perhaps closer to dead people than to me at that moment. Closer to ghosts. I couldn't understand where he was, how someone could be so lost to me when he was standing so near. I'm here. I'm here, he laughed, but that made it worse. I can see those pink lights on the mountains.

The problem was that he'd been that way for many

hours. It wasn't passing. A trip that never ended. Dropped some purple hearts in the guest house the previous evening, Chandra said, and then Fred had started dancing. He's on another planet, Chandra added philosophically, but he's not coming down. I think he's flipped.

Some people had tried to explain it: flexing walls, pulsing ceilings, transfiguring clouds. Colours that smelled sharp or sweet, sounds that rang out from the lurid skies. But looking at his sweaty hair and the broken happiness on his face, he was a locked-in mystery, as peculiar as the inner world that every person carries inside. I wanted to know what he was seeing and to share the trip with him. I felt shut out. I'm not sorry, he said, jigging some more on the tabletop. There was no music but it was as if he was hearing it, dancing without end, moving endlessly to some secret rhythm.

What do we do if he's flipped out? I said to Anton. There were stories of psychiatric hospitals in the bigger cities in Pakistan, places where they held people in padded cells. A consultant with a degree from Europe pieced brains back together. Someone said they'd seen the patients parading in a courtyard in Lahore, all wearing the same white hospital gowns, their skinny legs sticking out underneath. Other people said the high commission helped when people cracked up; they arranged matters when flip-outs got out of hand, when their friends couldn't handle it anymore. There were things that could be done – enema sedatives, possibly handcuffs, bundling people into aeroplanes, where they would be given three seats in the row to themselves. The high commission would send out a junior guy in a car in the first instance to take a look, and if it was grim enough, then they would make the arrangements. Bad for Britain's reputation, the guy with the moustache said, too many British kooks flipping out. A girl said she knew someone who'd faked it just to get the passage home. But if he'd needed that – if Fred had gone that far – we'd have had to call his father.

Fred was whirling in the street now, making for the edge of the road, and vehicles swerved slightly in anticipation of him falling in the road. He looked drunk, and a couple of guys beeped their horns and jeered. Then he saw a building site and made for a wall, half built and abandoned by the bricklayers who'd gone off for their break and left the trowels with their plumb lines of string. The bamboo scaffold was lacking right angles, offbeat squares and sagging in places, all relying on stringy knots. It looked as if it wouldn't hold the weight of a cat. He picked over their equipment and buckets quickly, and then, hoisting himself up on the edge of the scaffold, he started to climb. No, I said in a voice which was clear and firmer than I'd ever known it, Fred come down. But he was spirited, dizzy but also reinforced with some kind of inhuman energy which propelled him upwards, his long legs working up the rungs two at a time. He was at least fifteen feet up by now. I looked to Anton, should I follow him? But the danger was transparent, and also Fred's speed and determination. One or two of the Afghans had come out of the café by now, a couple chuckling, but their voices turning to fear, shouting up at him in Pashto, the pitch was rising all around.

When I think back on that now, I imagine he was thinking he could fly. Like Icarus, driven up to a cliff. He was seeing wings of gold-and-white feathers on his arms, he was seeing himself soaring and swooping. Hold him, will you? I ordered Anton, who was making his way to the scaffolding. I ran out into the road and stood in front of the most expensive-looking car I could see, which bumped to a halt. You have to help me. My friend. He's not well, he's very sick. We need an ambulance.

Big Red had helped Anton, talked him down from the ladder, and then he'd tackled Fred's ankles, knocking him down to the ground, restraining him with his lumberjack muscles and his enormous legs.

The Indian doctor came, which was to her credit, although she didn't hurry. She had on a white coat over her sari, rolls of flesh under the blouse, with a leather handbag slung over her shoulder. It took two of them to pin Freddie down in the end, the Irish boys helped, and then she produced a syringe, shook it, and raised it to the light. I admired her theatricality.

Don't let them take me. Don't let them. The wailing, the painful cries that he made as they took him away. No sign of Chandra, we wouldn't see him for dust after that.

Should we tell Fred's father? I asked Anton as we waited outside the hospital later that afternoon, thinking of our friend who was locked inside. Best not to, said Anton. I am sure I was considering what was best for Fred, but I can also admit, after all these years, that I did have an itch of curiosity too. I was quite keen on ringing up Fred's father. Possibly making myself better known to him, assuring him that I was doing everything possible for his son. After all, it was likely we would get to know each other better in future years, wasn't it? Perhaps I was too emphatic. Joyce – honestly – best not to call him. Anton was firm.

The doctor said it would take a few days for him to settle down. But he'd be OK. It's a classic flip-out. She seemed to know what she was doing. The doctor said they see a couple of westerners every month and their job was – how did she put it? – shutting the stable door after the horse has bolted.

14

They held him in some sort of room, minimally furnished, soft padding on the walls. The place was cool and quiet inside, the finest hospital in Kabul. Nurses in starched white bibs and a matron with a heavy watch and polished shoes. Fred's doctor had been educated in Bombay. Only the wealthiest Afghans could afford the place, that was obvious from the cars which pulled up outside; the staff were kind, professional, equipped with the latest in medical knowledge. Thank Christ for Fred's credit card.

On our first visit the doctor suggested that we take Fred to the garden, and we walked with him slowly, waiting for him to speak. He was wearing a tartan dressing gown with a tasselled cord, which belonged to the hospital. The patients in the courtyard looked in a much worse state than Fred, one in a wheelchair, catatonic, staring into the electric blue sky, members of distinguished families kept hidden from sight.

So let's sit over here, mates, shall we? Sorry about all

the brouhaha. He pulled out a Rothmans. Looking great, Fred, Anton lied. They've fed me up good and proper. It has all passed, settled down in the past day. I can't remember anything after Bamiyan actually. He seemed calmer, less frenetic, though shaken with the thoughts of wherever he'd been, wherever he'd nearly flown. When we left, Anton stood and circled his arms around him, and it was good to see the two of them like that, reunited, recognising how much they needed each other. Can you bring me my guitar? He asked on our third visit, and that was when I knew that he'd turned a corner.

The final visit – I guess he was there for about ten days in the end – we went with good news, and he sat in the sunshine and picked out a few chords, slowly, not a recognisable song. We wanted to tell you first, to let you know, they've said they'll discharge you tomorrow morning. We'll come and get you.

Fred's flip-out. Nowadays they'd call it drug-induced psychosis. After the flip-out, Fred started relying on me much more. While he was in hospital, I'd gone through all his things; I'd washed his clothes and I'd taken his backpack, emptied it out and reorganised it. A little peek at those letters that Trixie had given him? I hadn't forgotten about that precious bundle. It might have crossed my mind, but the rumpled manila envelope was not there, alas. I bought him soap and a new plastic comb. The dhobi did a decent job; the clothes were pressed under a hot iron, and all his long shirts and baggy pants were in a fresh pile. He'd returned to us. He still smoked but he took a step back from the other dope, he was really trying to get sober. He slept late but he'd come down around eleven and do yoga, manically, sun salutations on repeat, and then he'd eat like a horse, scooping flatbread in sauce with his fingers. He was really trying.

I began to think of myself as the watchman or the bodyguard of my boys. And they started to act like I was too: Joycie, can you look after this? Anton would say, with a parcel or a bag. And I liked the responsibility. And with Vera too, they began to see that I understood, that I could lift the bonnet and make suggestions. Or barter a price for a room. I was much better at it than Freddie, although that wasn't hard. All that education that they'd had in that school, the hours with their beaks, all that Cicero and Virgil and Plato, all those plummy house debates, yet they hadn't been taught the things that I'd picked up since leaving school: how to balance a cash register, how to check an invoice, how to change a fuse. A hell of a lot of money down the drain on school fees, if you looked at it like that. Fred would always land sunny side up. The old pile would be his one day, there'd be a bride and babies and Labradors, surely, because that was always how it worked out for his kind. That wasn't as simple for me. I had to stay ready to defend myself, on my mettle. I was vigilant.

Sometimes – and perhaps this sounds curious – I imagined myself in that house in Gloucestershire, Anton had described it so well. And when he told me about the problem with the damp, or the way they'd employed carpenters to repair the mezzanine in the chapel, I remembered my brother and his mates and thought about what might be done in such a place with some determination. And I began, perhaps, to picture myself as the lady of that house, drawing open the drapes in the morning to see the view down to the lake, or waiting for a maid to arrive with a breakfast tray and to sweep them open for me. You see, that sort of place needs a woman like me, someone practical who can deal with craftsmen and staff. A lot of those houses go to rot these days because the families who own them come and go from holidays in the Caribbean; they forget about the work it takes to keep a place like that going, the pointing between the brickwork and the sensitive restoration of the plaster. Fred and I would have made a wonderful pair in that sense, because he could have carried on with his music. I wouldn't have minded if he spent all day in the studio, weeks on tour even, we could have had a barn converted into a recording studio. I would have been waiting there for him, patiently, overseeing the details of the house, ordering the servants to lay out a late-night spread for his rockstar friends, smoked salmon and thick slices of buttered bread. They'd have come in exhausted and happy to eat and drink in the farmhouse kitchen, kicking their biker boots onto the oak chairs, saying, Goodness, Fred, what would you do without Joyce? When I think back to us then, I feel sorry about the way that things ended up.

Anton asked me the week that Fred was discharged from hospital, should we carry on? Is there a risk to Fred? Will he lose it again, silly bugger? He might not handle India, it's wilder than here, we can get a flight, he said. Fly out from Peshawar or Lahore? There's no need to press on. There was a kind of unspoken underwriting. We all knew that if the going got tough Fred could call the governor. Anton didn't want to do that, but it was a security blanket. Even when we were muddling through by ourselves; he'd have signed a cheque.

Anton's heart wasn't in the idea of turning back home. But it was good of him to ask. No way, I said. I'd had a chat with the doctor who confirmed my hunch, that these kind of crack-ups aren't all that rare. Most kids took about a week to recover and then got back on the road again. Their brains reassembled themselves, synapses started doing the right thing. If they kept off the psychoactive substances, looked after themselves better. Make sure he sleeps, she said, as if I could do anything about Fred's nocturnal habits.

So Anton and I trod carefully with Fred when he re-emerged. Will you both stop treating me with kid gloves? he said, but he said it with a smile. And then, oi, Antonios, bring me a cup of chai. We did step carefully. We suggested walks – Anton took him out to the botanical gardens – we made sure we didn't stay out too late. Chandra slunk off somewhere, with his tail between his skinny little legs. We drew a protective circle around Fred, didn't let the hardcore freaks get too close to him.

We kept tabs on him, and Fred had changed. He cut back on the womanising, started reading. First he borrowed a couple of books from Anton, mostly bizarre spiritual tracts, then he started picking them up at the guest houses, exchanging them with others. He particularly liked *Siddhartha* by Herman Hesse and carried it around like a talisman. You should try meditating, he said to me one day, and now and then he really could be found completely still in the lotus position, his eyes closed, bringing back some core of himself to order.

Have you heard Fred play lately? Anton said to me one morning as he spooned honey over his pancakes. He's coming out with some miraculous shit. That was high praise from Anton and that evening I said, Fred, sing me something. We were in the garden of the Faloodah Guest House, and there were a few other travellers around, playing backgammon, one man tapping out a long-stemmed pipe. Fred played – he was always happy to play – and what had changed was that he was writing his own songs now, not just playing other people's tunes, poetry, words and music entwined like leaves and flowers, melodies that I couldn't shake from my head and words that kept coming back in poignant phrases. A whole level up from your usual strummer, so even on his guitar, which was looking a bit worse for wear, and had been painted by some chick in hideous swirls, the sound was magical. The other travellers came over, their games forgotten; it was impossible to ignore that music.

They are good, you can make a living from those songs, Fred, honestly, I said to him afterwards, and he lay back and put his head on my lap like a little boy. He showed me then: he had lyrics, pages of them, one on the back of a napkin, others scribbled into the margins of an address book. I teased out some small tangles from his hair with my fingers. You know what, Joyce, I'll tell you a secret. For the first time ever, I think they are good, and he opened his eyes and smiled up at me. And I felt then it was certain that he'd be famous, that everyone in the world would know those songs one day too, that they'd be cut into the grooves of LPs and found in teenage bedrooms, and that Fred's music was going to spread out into the world, and that Anton and I had played our own not inconsiderable part. I was becoming very focused on our future. You need someone powerful, a manager or a record company? I didn't know what I was talking about, but I'd picked up the odd bits from music magazines. All in good time, my dearest, he said, and kissed my hand. And I was ambitious for him – I didn't want anything for myself, did I? – it was all about his talent.

I started to wonder if Fred was growing up. And if there might be something real between us. Since he'd come out of the hospital, I'd had a deep yearning for him which came on like an illness. I wanted him. I can say with certainty I had never wanted a man like that. But I let my head overrule matters. Because at the same time, I disapproved of him severely. It took all my willpower sometimes not to just agree, let him slip into my room, under my mosquito net, let his brown, bitten legs curl against mine. It would be a mistake, it would complicate everything. There is no way you are sleeping with Fred, young lady, I reprimanded myself in my mother's voice, seeing a wagging finger. And do not get too drunk near him either, you silly little floozie. You keep those knickers up. I guess my inner voice could be a little harsh.

It was the future I was working towards. All in good time, he had promised. I was convinced he was talking about us. In my head I had decided that it would be better for us to get together back in England, when he would fully realise what a pair we made. What would Anton think? He was Fred's best friend, I grant him that. But

I knew I saw something else that even Anton missed. At times I felt I knew him like no one else, and I knew I would be the only one to save him.

He wrote a song for me around then, in Kabul, and I pretended it was just an everyday thing. A gentle melody, some eastern influences in the mix, a touch of George Harrison, perhaps. I said, oh, that's so nice, Fred, it's so sweet, and nodded and clapped to the melody, when inside my heart was bursting.

Do you think the tripping did it? Opened up something in his neural pathways? His music is so much better, I said to Anton one day after listening to him perform. You sound like Chandra, he responded. Where did Chandra go to, by the way? Funny how he just disappeared. So much for Fred's best buddy, I muttered. Something in the way Anton looked away made me think that he'd had a hand in it. Did you say something to him? I told him I'd report him to the local police for possession, said Anton, if I ever saw him anywhere near Fred again.

15

That was about the time we decided to take the road down into Pakistan, to cross the Khyber Pass. We'd been waiting for the right moment. I wasn't sure if it was meteorological or mechanical. Perhaps it was something in the stars by that point. But we waited and waited for the right day. Anton said it had to be perfect. We all needed to be in the proper frame of mind, he said.

In Kabul we couldn't be alone for long. We were all on pretty much the same route, there were only so many digs to stay in. So even though we were crossing the world, there was a small world on the overland, its own little bubble, the same faces and names and rumours recirculated and resurfaced. At the Faloodah Guest House, several old faces appeared with news of others, greeted like long-lost friends.

Everyone was looking a little jaded: five o'clock shadows and tatty clothes. As for me, well, I still put my best foot forward. I still made sure I plucked my eyebrows. You could have still found me at the GPO. Black eyeliner rimmed under the eyes, I was an unremarkable twenty-four-year-old. Plain Jane. My ordinariness, that was my best feature, as it happens; it helped me to see the little things that others couldn't, gave me a good vantage point, I could stand in Freddie's shadow, by his side, without the other girls getting jealous. The ones with gamine faces or Farrah Fawcett hair barely noticed me or thought they could elbow me out the way, to get a seat at the table with my boys. I was the one they trusted. I was the one my boys came back to.

There was a convoy of us the week in November we decided to leave for the Khyber Pass, and it was that we would move as a group. We'd been warned about hairpins and gunrunners. So all of us set off at dawn that morning from Jalalabad: a bus chartered from London, three Land Rovers including Vera, an old Ambassador and the VW with the West Berliners. We must have looked quite the flotilla.

I am sick as a dog, Fred declared that morning. Loops and switchbacks and climbing upwards, the land was studded with fortresses and walls, anonymous, as if enemies waited everywhere in the hills. Fred's guts were a mess and he was quiet, asking only to stop once to puke out of the car door. Dry retching, very little came up. I felt he was holding on for the toilet, his innards in turmoil, and that made the whole drive uncomfortable for all of us, knowing that he was squirming in pain, unable to appreciate the view.

A fabled place. More a name than a place. We found a small shack, a traveller's rest that was adapting to freaks, with a hot samovar, and a toilet at the back – a door and hole, and Fred spent at least half an hour in there. Came out pale but more at ease. He was only passing water by now, nothing left in him, and I kept handing him the drinking canister to try and keep him hydrated. I was looking out for him.

The men in those parts were always carrying guns and trussed up with bandoliers, as if they perpetually expected trouble. As if our men might bring trouble! Just had to look at the state of our guys! We were all standing around, waiting for Fred, drinking tea and talking gradients, altitudes and gears; the Berliners were getting twitchy, keen to reach India as quickly as possible, and so we told them to press on – we'd be OK – and watched the rest of the colourful caravan proceed on without us. We'd be an hour behind them; we might even catch them up, we lied.

Then more climbing ever upwards, and we willed Vera on, she was only in second gear but holding out. I took a turn at the wheel and let Fred lie down in the back, though it didn't help. By lunchtime we'd reached the pass itself, the frontier, as low as a river bed tucked between magnificent ranges on either side. We stopped the van to take pictures. Fred didn't get out the back to look. It's the Khyber-fucking-Pass, said Anton. Fred, you have to come and have a look. You have to see it. Fuck the fucking Khyber Pass, said Fred, groaning, and we didn't bother him again. We stood there, quite alone, looking back down the valley which was laid out beneath us. Not timeless, but somehow no one's, not for the taking or the owning, the road was one long snake. I can't say I liked it much. It was fighting country. I'd hoped I might pick up a souvenir but there was not one single thing to buy.

I knew Anton wanted to be awed too, but really what

he loved was civilisation. Paintings done with a single horsehair, geometric tiles. Courtly details. He told me about the men who had passed through here; Darius the Great, Babur, Kipling. The Great Game. But they were all old stories and the rocks didn't speak. So we didn't linger too long, slammed the doors and started the descent, out of Afghanistan and down to Peshawar.

Fred's first night in Peshawar was just as bad, nothing but a few sips of water passed his lips that evening, and I was starting to think about a doctor when he came down the next morning to have breakfast looking brighter, and broke off a corner of bread. I am on the mend, he announced.

We skirted Islamabad, dodging Felicity, who hovered over the city as we drove by, sped down to Lahore as quickly as possible. We were all very focused on India by this point, and Pakistan felt like an obstacle in the way, this new country with its inconvenient borders, its founder's stern face bearing down on us at every corner. We were descending now, losing height, heading towards the plains.

The next day I was washing myself off, removing the grit of the journey with a bucket wash, right over the head from a plastic bucket, lovely if you've never tried it, when I heard a shrill, angry bleating. The sound intensified – I stopped soaping my hair – to a pitch of great, angry misery. A wail that was spine-chilling. I felt strange standing there naked, hearing that wail. What the hell was that? I said to Anton when I was back in the courtyard, did you hear it? Wouldn't go outside if I were you. It's Bakir Eid. It was Sacrifice-a-Goat Day. We'd seen them the night before in the street, with bows and ribbons round their necks, fluffy little goats, brushed up and petted. Fred came in then, ashen faced – Good grief, it's a murder scene out there. He'd seen a man grab a goat by its horns and slice its throat across. There was blood on every pavement. He sat down and re-lit a beedi, holding half an inch tight between his thumb and forefinger. Anton tried with great patience to explain to us the meaning behind it. Fred had no truck with any of it.

Later that afternoon the smell of the barbeque came wafting over the city, crispy and succulent; the family who owned the place came in, dressed up to the nines, with a tray of chops and skewers and piles of freshly baked bread and it was the most delicious thing I ate in Pakistan. But Fred shook his head and refused it quite rudely and sulked while we all ate. He hates the sight of blood, Anton said to me later on, as if I didn't already know. He can't stand it, it's a sort of phobia with Fred. Pansy, he said, winking at me. The next day when I walked out of the guest house I saw the blood running in the gullies, along the edges of the kerb, diluted but clearly still blood, mixed with all the other dust and muck from the street. Cloudy blood that had been brushed off the pavement and into the road. The same colour red as our warning lights.

PART 5

GRAND TRUNK ROAD

16

The crossing between Pakistan and India wasn't as big a deal as we had expected. What an anticlimax, Fred said, same food, same people, different signs and symbols. Anton started talking about the Partition of 1947, and all those refugees, which I'd never actually heard about at that point in my life, and the change from the swirling Arabic script to the compact strokes of Hindi, and Fred hit him over the head with a bunch of bananas. Give it a break, Boff, but they were laughing, and Anton started talking about a teacher who'd thrown fruit at Fred when he didn't know the answer to test questions, and Fred said, are you sure we had the same education? And it was probably about then that I decided that when I returned to England I might have a shot at studying myself, send off for a couple of prospectuses from further-education colleges, or at least take reading books a little more seriously than I had up until that point, which is something I am proud to say I have pursued.

As we roared towards India, Fred played the horn for

fun and barged through the middle of the traffic, scattering cyclists who swerved just quickly enough, and the cows nodded on the roadsides or nosed their way along the side. And things were a blur of shacks and dried-out houses as the road became something else entirely: flat, green fields of sugar cane, and endless long roads again, the roads straighter and cutting across crops so there was always a villager in sight, with a plough or walking by the edge of the road. It was better down here on the plains, it felt safer, a place that had drawn people in for thousands of years, Anton said, coming for the rivers and the good soil. Rivers came and went in glimpses, often along the road, huge and milky brown, and the hundreds of people washing and whacking laundry on the banks.

The locals mattered to us only insomuch as they served us – they were the backdrop to our play. And occasionally you'd meet someone who had studied in the west or who wanted to talk about the great classics of English literature, of which I was horribly ignorant at that time. Mostly they were there in the background, to sweep and fetch and cook and carry and drive and open and close and till their lands, as if everyone had just been there waiting in the wings for us to turn up and start the show. They made for great photographs, and Anton took pictures of street children with matted hair, men stirring cauldrons at the tanneries or – a classic favourite – women with pots or bundles of firewood balanced perfectly on their heads. Did they exist without us there? It wasn't clear to me. And did they care about us? I wondered. They stared with curiosity, sometimes with concern, rarely with reproach. And the same conversations went round in circles over the tables of the guest houses: how to haggle hard and never overpay, as it set a precedent for those who followed behind you on the trail; which salads and fruit to avoid, what the policy was on giving to beggars.

Admittedly, we weren't *very* curious about the people we were seeing – but you couldn't help notice. We saw it all, the poverty, folks without limbs, children living on the roadside. The thing was, what could any of us do? What could you say about it, really, that didn't end up as one massive downer? We were unable to explain what we saw. We didn't know why we came from homes with hot running water and cellophane packets of cornflakes and so many cars and more-or-less functioning schools, and why these other folks didn't. We were the world's winners, I guess, if I'd had to put it in stark terms. Things were simpler then, when Britain was still on top.

We blew the budget in Amritsar, a colonial bungalow in the civil lines with white colonnades and a verandah, owned by the widow of a Sikh brigadier. It had seen better days. She took one look at us and said she didn't want any riff-raff and we let Anton do the talking and he brought her round. We could have pulled strings, opened Fred's address book, but he was chary of any more family encounters after the stay in Tehran with Trixie and Guy. The old lady, Mrs Kaur, warmed to us. She served gin after six o'clock and insisted that as it was winter, we must have hot-water bottles in our beds and cocoa before we went up to our rooms. A servant brought the mugs on a tea tray, and Mrs Kaur asked us how many spoons of sugar we wanted and served us herself. The smell of cocoa took me to London, and for a moment I looked at us in that drawing room, with pictures of old turbaned regiments on the wall, and didn't know what we were doing there, how we could have possibly ended up there. I thought of my childhood and how I had never been prepared for this kind of world. Mrs Kaur saw me looking at the walls, and she said, quite kindly, there's a wedding in a village tomorrow, you'd like to come with me to a wedding, yes? I turned the gold ring on my finger.

Mrs Kaur didn't like taking no for an answer, although the arrangements were loose, and we weren't exactly sure whose wedding it was, someone in the wider household, I think, perhaps the cook's daughter; Mrs Kaur made it very clear that she had made a handsome contribution to the costs and that we could come at her bidding. It was settled.

Don't smoke at the wedding, Fred, OK? Anton said, as we waited for the bus the next morning. I know how to behave, Fred said. Yeah, but this wedding isn't in the home counties. They have their own way of doing things. I was nervous, truth be told. I didn't much like the idea of a wedding where the girl had never seen the boy before. Not a great excuse for a party.

The bus came, a rattling old can, exactly at ten as Mrs Kaur had predicted. She didn't have room in her Ambassador for us, or perhaps her invitation to hippies like us seemed rash in the light of day. There were no freaks on board; we were the only foreigners. Mostly Indian students and a businessman in a nylon shirt and villagers taking back bags to the village and a woman in a sari with a few live chickens in a cage. The bus driver was accompanied by another guy who perched at the back, half hanging out of the rear door, hitting the side of the bus and yelling out to the main driver. They appeared to take it in turns to take on this role, switching up the driving. The businessman was helpful in his rigid textbook English and said he'd make sure we were deposited at the right place, and Fred was good as his word and stayed off the cigs and the weed, and asked the man about agricultural yields in a surprisingly plausible way – comparing notes about livestock and the soil of England – so the man took care to make sure we were let down at exactly the right place and instructed a young kid to lead us to the wedding.

The memories of that wedding today are blurred, a lot of the details were hard for us to follow; hundreds of people milled about, and the events seemed to go on all day without much structure or sense of what we should do, or when we might escape. It was all outside in a village courtyard, with the brown dust held at bay by ribbons and tinsel decorations, and children who had been wiped clean with wet rags, pulled into tight hairstyles. Tureens of dal and rice and piles of sweets and the girl, in red, sitting demurely with her gaze down near a pile of things, stacked high, a bed frame, and crockery, and a Phillips radio still in the cardboard box, which had been formally presented by Mrs Kaur. We should have brought a gift, said Anton, berating himself. Fred fixed it by taking out some rupee notes – he'd somehow even procured an envelope – and gave the money to the bride and groom, with a flourish and a bow, and perhaps a little speech, and Mrs Kaur watched on approvingly.

The thing I remember most of all that day was a nasty little incident as we were leaving, some sort of fuss to the side of the road. Jostling, someone brought ahead from within the crowd, pushed forwards by eager relatives. A man stepped out, straight-backed, asking for something. In a patterned cap, pastel pinks and greens, his face speckled with grey stubble. Wrinkled as a peanut shell. Bare feet, horrible toenails. He stood there with a piece of paper in his hand, folded so many times the creases could have dissolved it into pieces. He handed it to Anton and I looked over his shoulder.

Some sort of service record, crossed swords at the top of the letter, registration numbers, papers from the Gurkha Rifles. He's an old soldier, said Anton. I knew he was asking for something but I couldn't figure out what. The crowd pressed in and a small girl took my hand. The little girl's palm was rough and tender at the same time, it had the texture of a foot's sole. One small hard louse near the parting of her scalp. The old man was quiet, but his son seemed angry. He was even raising his voice a little. We didn't understand and then Anton twigged. He fought in all our old wars. We didn't know how we could help him. We shrugged and looked apologetic. I dug around in my backpack as if I could find something there, but there were only a couple of old bananas. And Fred again came to the rescue by producing some rupees, but somehow it lacked the excitement of his gift to the couple, and it didn't seem to satisfy the man although he nodded politely and didn't refuse the notes.

And the second scene I remember, seeing the bride as she was leaving; close-up she looked about the same age as her teenage husband, in elaborate red skirts and paper-flower garlands. Scenes as she said goodbye to her parents, to her sister, who cried and wouldn't let go of her until the driver had to intercede with the mother to tear them apart, to prise her hands, her thin wrists stacked with bangles, from her sister, who fell on the floor as if a disaster had befallen them. I forgot this episode completely until I sat down to write about it today. Unhappy brides, the world over! How much better off I have been living by myself, never having to deal with any of that nonsense, and keeping my dignity intact.

The next morning, back in the city, we found the Amritsar General Post Office, a jolly building, gaudy in red and black paint. Anton and I were sitting under a tree on the lawns in front of the building. Our letters were on display, behind a grille like little miracles, and the postmaster fetched a key and opened up the lock for us.

My own folks were sending letters dutifully, my mother writing in her neat way with news about Clive mostly, and his wife and their plans for Christmas. Christmas! It was already late November. Did we plan to be back by then? It seemed like a fairy tale from where I was sitting. The fruitcake and the coloured strings of electric lights being wound around the tree. Dates and seasons didn't make sense anymore. After three pages, the tone changed abruptly. The talk of the town, my mother wrote, was that my ex-husband, Tom, still my husband at that point, had been arrested. He'd done over a man in the town, a nasty brawl in the local pub. I hadn't thought of that place for months, could feel at once the sticky tabletops and hear the clanging for last orders. There'd been a trivial dispute, they had taken it outside to the kerbside, except he'd kept a pint glass in his hand, and used it to smash the other man hard over the head.

I stopped reading and held the letter away from me, perplexed. You OK, Joycie? asked Anton, who was sealing up his own aerogrammes. Yeah, kind of. I went on reading. A pity when a nice lad can't control himself, she went on. You'd expect it from workers at the factory, that kind of behaviour, not from a man with his own business. With responsibilities. People always said he was going places; he wore a tie. There was no mention of what had happened to me that night, she'd never addressed it, but that letter was as good as an acknowledgement. I touched the scar under my chin.

I thought for the first time without shame that I had done the right thing. I thought of my father there, his tweed cap in his hands, and the way he'd collected me from the house when I had called, and stood his ground with Tom, although he was a big lad, built like a brick shithouse. And how he had carried my suitcase for me to the car and opened the door for me, demonstrating how a gentleman behaved. It was like watching another version of myself, and I felt proud of the girl who had never considered, even for a moment, and even when others suggested otherwise, staying. It was just the once, pet, my mother had whispered, in hope.

I thought about how Tom and I got together. I'd not said no. And sometimes I'd felt it was uncomfortable and heavy and I was pinned under, and sometimes I liked him and the weight of him pressing down on me. And then it became normal and I was more willing, and then it seemed like marriage should follow, because sooner or later I was going to mess it up and get up the duff and I wanted to be somewhat in control of my own destiny, and it seemed to me that no man I'd actually chosen to kiss could control me more than my own parents. Those were the sort of elemental mistakes.

Look at this, I said to Anton, and handed it over for him to read. It was easier than explaining it myself. He let out a long exhalation as he read the letter, turning over the page and studying it with scholarly attention. We were sitting on the earth, and ants scuttled this way and that around our ankles. Well done on getting out of there, he said, and offered me a hand, pulling me up from the ground. I told Anton then. How I went flying backwards from the countertop. The ceiling was in front of me, the kitchen lights were dazzling. A kitchen scene, the blood could have been ketchup; it all happened, it seemed to me, in a silence, in a vacuum, with no time before or after it. Joyce, you fell, Tom had said as he rushed to me and held me like a child who had fallen down. He was at the tap, dabbing a towel, pressing it against my bruised skin, hushing me, making as little noise as possible. On his knees, picking up broken shards. A stupid accident, everyone agreed. It was only a few stitches. The GP told me to buck up. But I knew I hadn't fallen, and I knew I had every right to be upset. I'd married a bastard.

The day after I had the stiches removed, I saw the advert in the *Standard*.

17

There was often a bit of tension in the cab about driving now, you had to have your wits about you on the Grand Trunk Road; no snoozing at the wheel. Plenty of unsolicited comments from the passenger seat. Anton thought that Fred was erratic – which was true – and Anton's mind drifted away from the lane, every so often, so we lurched to the side. They both liked it if I took over, spared them the squabbles. We'd all heard the story about the Indian drivers who ran people over in broad daylight and kept going, never slowed. They dragged bodies along, because they feared the wrath of the mob. Villagers unleashing rough justice on the reckless fellow before the police had even caught wind of the crash. Beating him to death with those long sticks they call lathi, taking revenge for their kin on the rich folks who motored through, razing little people to the ground. Anton was more worried about running over a cow. That's real trouble, he said, that's heavy.

Sometimes when I think back on the journey down from Punjab I get muddled, and I wonder if the place names that I remember are accurate, if I have got the order correct. I know that one day Anton insisted we stop at a fortress out on some higher ground; I think it was the day we were heading towards Delhi, somewhere on the outskirts of the city.

There were no other tourists, so the local guides sprung to life when they saw us coming and we were ambushed by two rivals competing for our full attention. The English suffered mightily here, madam, said one. Let me show you. The site of an uprising, where there had been a terrible rebellion which nearly overthrew the colonials. The English people had been stuck there for weeks waiting for soldiers to come and free them. We were unable to shake the guides off. They were insistent, ducking and diving between us, and so one man, the younger one, who seemed to have won against his competitor, went into a long-prepared spiel about the siege and the battle to save the Brits.

Anton added to it with his own stock of stories; a tragic picture, Cawnpore and ladies flung down to their deaths in wells, soldiers liberating those who were besieged for many weeks, eking out the last grains, trying to get word from home. We looked gloomily at the cannonball marks on the side of the walls. We were invited to imagine the fear of the ladies in frocks as they waited for news and, when I stepped down into a low stairwell, dried old grass on the floor, I felt how the walls must have squeezed, closing around the women, while their men were out with their muskets on the battlefields, some hundreds of miles away – it must have been a torture, I said, imagine being stuck down here, trying to protect your kids. The food started to run out and we understood how petrifying it was, unsure of the loyalty of those they had trusted to run their baths and cook their food and even those servants still with them, even those ayahs holding their babies, unsure if they were willing on the rebels, smirking to themselves. Perhaps that was the worst of it – not knowing who you might trust anymore, so far from home.

When we came out at the entrance to the site, the other guide had reappeared. The two men got in an argument – something about licences and trespassers and the right to show us around. The first man, the guide we had started with, kept brandishing his pass, which was stamped and signed with the official Archaeological Survey of India seal, while the other man remonstrated loudly. We didn't know what the hell was going on. Eventually the official guide relented, and the other man stepped forward. Come with me please, sirs. We walked some distance from the neat and well-maintained site of the fort towards some scrubland, trees and overgrown grass, and I started to feel nervy, as if this was some kind of trap, like all the stories we had been hearing, of capture and encirclement. This tree here, sir. We looked up at the tree, knotty overground roots. An ancient tree, large and looming over us. This is where my grandfather was hung. Indians were hung? Madam, plenty. No trial. Just hung. These are not on the signboards, not in the guidebooks. I might have muttered something about hokum. I wasn't pleased to see Anton upstaged by this man. Not one bit. We had gone off script. This area didn't feature on the map that he held out in front of him. Give the guy a chance, said Fred, amused by the scene.

The man was in his seventies and had a grey beard. He said he was born in the time of Queen Victoria. That his grandfather was a mutineer, a servant who had sneaked explosives from the armoury, that his grandmother was a widow. The dates were plausible. He wanted us to know all these things, that was clear by the way he spoke.

We looked up at the old tree – a banyan, he told us – and the strong branches that might have held bodies. I never liked the look of banyans, their tangled roots pale snakes the wrong way up, hiding all the dark secrets. And afterwards, Anton said it was the most interesting part of the whole day. I liked that old chap a lot, he said, I take back some of my words. That fellow has really got me thinking. History isn't just a list of facts, he said, it's not just beads on a chain. To be sure, there are the immovables, the hard dates, deaths. But the way you can spin things this way and that. Things are up for grabs, you know, Joyce?

Well, I wasn't best pleased, I must say. That was when I realised Anton didn't always get it right, even when he assumed his professorial airs and graces. That Anton's version might be argued with, this was all quite a revelation, I can tell you. I'd looked up to Anton quite a lot by this point, as you may have noticed, and I liked the idea of someone who knew everything, delivering some hard truth about these places which were a jumble of confusion. Anton should have just stuck to his guns, defended his version to that man, who might have been a con artist in any case. And I wanted him to be better than the local guides, who all the travellers said overcharged and couldn't be trusted at all because they hassled people for tips, and worked on hearsay and rumour, and had plainly never had a sniff at a decent education. So I kept my mouth shut; but that was Anton to a T, overcomplicating things and prodding at the past when it might have been better to just leave the agreed version well alone.

Rolling into Delhi was majestic. We were all keyed up. Alexander coming over the mountains, trains of splendour, camels and elephants on every side. The road opened up wider and wider to five lanes, six lanes, until we were in the heart of the city, breathing in the exhausts and the smell of hot fat. Everything we had already seen was here, condensed. Boiled. Multiplied. Louder music, carts and street vendors and paperback books laid out on sheets, dense-packed streets and carts with sacks too large to pull, and kids dodging the road, and horns and hooters and sadhus in saffron and the odd freak in dreads and beads and bare feet, ambling along oblivious. And the buildings. Monumental, in circles and circles of grass; we hadn't seen lawns like that for months, made green by decadent sprinklers. Everything was big, the city shouted out power. Anton slapped Fred on the back and I thought we had bounced back. That we had made it. It felt like they might be repairing their bond, that by getting here we had actually achieved something. I am going to get wasted tonight, said Fred, leaning his head back on the headrest, and for once we all agreed. Let's find a hotel.

Fred paid for gin and tonics at the Imperial with his credit card, which was run off in triplicate on a solid machine. Each drink was about three days' daily expenditure. They tasted good and we downed them quickly. Fred didn't want to leave, so we bought one large beer with some remaining rupees and shared it between the three of us, demanded extra nuts.

Two women in saris sat at a nearby table and glanced over at us, trying not to stare. Their saris looked expensive, even to the untrained eye, and the more I looked at them the more I saw gold and small, discreet gems, rings, nose studs. Their arms were smooth but for tiny bracelet watches and their hair was oiled in neat buns. One had a Louis Vuitton handbag. I looked at my own feet, and the way the skin was cracking raw on my heels, and moved them deeper under the table.

I'm going to ask them for a light, said Fred. Anton groaned. Fred, there's a time and a place. Fred approached with his beedi and Anton and I watched him. His trousers had a rip on one side. He hadn't washed since the journey, I noticed. The younger one offered him a light from a heavy gold lighter, and stared at him. She spoke too quietly to hear. Gloucestershire, I heard Fred say, and then the older woman turned away, as if Fred was not there, ending the encounter.

Fred came back to us and the women glanced over and laughed, this time noticeably, staring right us. I couldn't be sure but I think one of them wrinkled her nose. Silly cows, I said. Sir, will you be wanting anything else? The maitre d'hotel was at our table, and standing square to the wall, ready for a scene. We'll be needing this table, soon, you see, sir. He was both apologetic and firm, and somehow we all stood up immediately and let him shepherd us out of that place, even Fred.

We made our way back to the Yes Sir Guest House.

That area, Paharganj, was a little slum for foreigners. Tucked alongside the railway sidings of New Delhi station, a bazaar ran along a dense main street with dubious back lanes, a place where drivers slept in their rickshaws, and other men hustled tickets and drugs and black market goods. The buildings were three or four storeys high, constructed illegally and covered in competing signboards. We saw pale tourists fresh from the airport and travellers coming to the end of the road haggling over a suitcase. The guest house was grimy, my room was windowless with one bare bulb.

Anton wasn't deterred. He explained that the advantage of Paharganj was being near the sights of Old Delhi and he led me out on foot, as if he was visiting an old haunt, and I realised that he had pictured Shahjahanabad so clearly in his mind, had visualised it already from his books, that he was determined to ignore the other inconvenient sights. He was in the seventeenth century, time travelling again, and reeling off the names of the great Mughal princesses and seeing grand processions into the city, the horses and elephants, and exotic sweetmeats and Persian poets. The metalworkers were at their streetside workshops, the heavy repetition of their hammers and chisels. Children on their haunches, hammering, coming to the end of a full day's work. I felt lucky that afternoon to be able to walk with Anton, protected by his confidence and as we elbowed our way through the crowds and came to the marble steps of the Jama Masjid, wide open and white, and then later, the best thing of all – he was almost leaping with excitement – the Lal Qila, its red walls and bastions towering over everything, gesturing to our insignificance.

Later, to get away from the crowds, we walked along the perimeter of the Red Fort's walls. As we walked further, the noise of the traffic receded, horns on the air, more distant now, and occasionally birds; dusk was falling, a hint of the breeze that was coming from the north. We stopped by a roadside tea stall and Anton bought two syrupy cups. We stood there on the roadside under a yellowing umbrella. Two drivers had got into a scrap, and the one with a lorry was raising his fist at the taxi driver blocking his way and the chaiwallah was shouting out something, adding his tuppenny bit, egging on the lorry man.

Anton said, he never mentions the situation. I wonder what he feels about it. The situation? The fifties. Those things that Trixie was harping on about. Fred's father was slap bang in the middle of it, Old Lord Carruthers. I don't know what you mean, I said. Anton blew on his steaming tea. The fight in the street had subsided and the tea-seller was back to stirring his pot.

Delhi was spread with pavement bookstalls, and the second-hand bookshops had knowledgeable owners. They could locate what you needed in seconds, dusting off the jacket as they pulled it down from a shelf. They had opinions, and ideas of their own, those booksellers. Anton had been reading everything he could about that colony. He'd found a copy of an investigation by a war correspondent, a report which made ripples at the time. He'd hid all this activity from Fred – and from me. He'd been on his own little quest in the book markets. If you go looking for trouble, you'll find it, in my view. Old rumours, the handiwork of a journalist, a thorn in the side of the British government. Anton got carried away. He couldn't help himself. Does Fred know? That you've been digging around all those old stories? I could tell from his look that Fred didn't have a clue. That it could get personal.

I was keen to know about the dashing earl, I longed to know about his house, his marriage, his art collection – but I wasn't prepared for what Anton told me that day. It was all just so... extraordinary. Anton conjured up some scenes from the 1950s, when Fred's dad was governor, which I found very hard to picture. Couldn't square it at all. It sounded more like a war zone. Communist rebels in the jungle. An emergency crackdown. The thing had just sort of spiralled, Anton said, some of the villagers were loyal to the British but many weren't. It was a game of chicken, trying to eliminate the trouble-makers. Finding them, pinning them down. Hard for the military to bring it under control, I mean it was much tougher than anyone could have anticipated, especially in the countryside. Fred was just a toddler. I can't believe he doesn't remember hearing about *any* of it, Anton said. The troops knew they might find themselves ambushed, unexpectedly isolated in the forests at nightfall. The earl had to clamp down. Decisive action from the top. A lot of the young guys swept into camps, behind barbed wire. Thousands of them. Guerilla types, vigilantes. The problem with that sort of situation is that you're not sure who is on your side, Anton explained, and I understood some of that from what we'd all heard about Vietnam. That was when Fred's mother decided to get out, Anton said. She commandeered a twin-prop from a military airfield, little Fred in one hand, a suitcase in the other. They went back to Gloucestershire, and his father followed six months later. All brought under control in a few years. Lord Carruthers is famous for winning the day.

And Fred doesn't remember any of it. He never wants to talk about it, so I stopped asking him a while back. For him life starts in England. Anyway, his dad acquitted himself as best he could. He looked away. Bit his lower lip.

Anton took my empty tea glass. He returned both glasses back to the man at the stall, who sluiced them out in a bucket of dirty dishwater. Do you know, he said, in school chapel we prayed for the armed forces? And once a man with epaulettes came to the sixth form common room to give us a lecture on leadership, about honour and how much can be achieved by a well-trained man, delivering the right word, the right nod.

What Anton told me that day made me admire Fred's family even more. Lord Carruthers was a hero! He'd been in charge of that great, well-known victory in the 1950s and I'd never even realised! Fred was far too modest about his family. Anton seemed to be hinting that Fred might have been disturbed by seeing that savagery around him. It must have been strange, for a little boy, to watch all those foreign men, with guns, paraded around a city in bloody uniforms. His mother was clearly sensible, to take him home at that point. Above all, however, I just felt proud to know the Carruthers.

18

The next day in Connaught Circus we wandered around for hours, lost in interlocking circles among the white pillars. The circle of hell, Anton called it. I was marvelling at the glass-fronted shops and the prices for imported Levis and hi-fi systems from Japan. We bought American-style shakes from a milk bar frequented by Indian university students, sat under the fans and listened to their highbrow conversation.

I saw the word 'war' in a newspaper headline, the *Times of India*. Things were hotting up in East Pakistan, the election had gone awry, India was embroiled; there were rumours of the border closing. The world was shifting under our feet, it felt like a premonition. All this talk of war and death. My faith in Fred's charm to get us through, to see us past border guards and soldiers, to produce the right amount of money or the right song. I had an unsettling sense that this might be misplaced. That maybe we couldn't always pull it off. That there was a limit to our luck. Fred's old money and ease in the world. What did it count for?

Delhi was good if you had money – AC cinemas and ice cream sundaes and light-up disco dancefloors – but terrible if you didn't. I know a lot of the travellers didn't care, but I minded the state of my hair and my nails and my worn-out jeans when I saw the ladies with their black oiled hair and their good handbags, and their sense of industry and purpose, off to work in Delhi's ministries and secretariats. Perhaps they were laughing at us, too, like the ladies in the Imperial Hotel.

Vera was parked up in Delhi, we'd paid a kid a few rupees to keep an eye on her. Going to be covered in monkey crap by the time we get back in, said Fred, but he was as relieved as Anton to give the driving a break.

My cash was running down the plughole and my mind was turning to home, to getting a return ticket. I was feeling sorry for myself, unable to purchase more items from the bazaar. Stories about how to make money were legion. We all carried so little but we all had something to sell – sell your jeans, sell your cassette tapes, sell your blood. For the junkies, it went further – rumours of blonde girls in cages in Bombay's backstreets, working for smack. Some overstayed visas, sold their passports to master forgers, ended up without papers, scared to go to an airport or tell anyone what they had done.

The best way to make money, the dream, was to appear in a Bollywood movie. You could get however many lakhs for a day as an extra, if you got a speaking part the rate shot up. There were rumours of the latest films and the demand for crowd scenes. Raj epics needed a lot of folks like us. Fred would have been perfect. You should try it, Fred, I urged him. He was interested, momentarily. Like I might get scouted in the street? he said. But mostly Fred was doing meditation and yoga at that point, and I felt conscious of my stiff limbs then, of my lack of pliability, as I saw him contorting in all those shapes. Sometimes you'd find yourself talking to his head, sometimes to his curved, arched back, as his head tucked under in a bow. At points Fred closed his eyes, while he bent and pressed his palms flat to the floor. He looked supple, a little other-worldly. I doubted he was listening to half of what I was saying about how he should find work in films. He was still smoking a lot – there were still infinite amounts of dope in Delhi. Come to think of it, he was probably overdoing the drugs again by that point. Beautiful fool.

A few arguments simmered about what to do next, where to go. Was reaching Nepal still realistic? Fred murmured something about holding out longer. We'd been on the road about four months. I figured I had enough to keep the trip going for a few more weeks, more if I sold my jeans. Anton wanted to see a couple of cities on the plains of Uttar Pradesh – Agra and Banaras, he was insistent about the Taj but somehow we were freaked by all the rumours of rip-offs and touts and cunning plans to trip up naïve travellers. Or maybe it just seemed like a tourist trap, too hackneyed; it couldn't be as good as it looked in the photographs. But Anton said we had to see something more of India, the real and ancient India, if we had gone all that way, that there was simply no way we could just loll about in Delhi, and he stood up to Fred for once and we agreed to go onwards, eastward, to Uttar Pradesh.

Dust had settled on the van and it had been a relief not to worry about the engine for a week or so. We needed to sell her in some sort of condition, not as a tin can. Vera's days with us were coming to an end, and before we left that morning Anton ran a hand along her flank. There was no way she'd manage the Himalayas. If we went up to the hills, we would be going by train. That much was clear. One more run, old girl, nearly there. We always talked of her as a girl, we still loved her, despite all the hassle she'd caused us. She looked worse for wear, dented and bruised. The boys liked to discuss how much they could get for her. A decent amount of rupees, I knew they'd give me a small share if I asked them, that was my insurance, but I didn't want to ask. It was their money. Would we split up? I could feel the possibility, a monsoon cloud gathering. Then one night I overheard the boys saying something about the trip up to Kathmandu. They were talking about a potential route. Booking tickets. They fell silent when they realised I was listening. I felt a sense of panic when I thought about us going our separate ways. That wasn't my plan at all. They couldn't just shake me off! Were the boys just going to abandon me? After all we'd been through together?

I heard the going rate for Levis was three hundred rupees. The Nepali guys loved them, apparently. I was serious about it, and washed them and dried them out on the balcony in the scorching sun, so they went crisp as cardboard. In the end, though, I couldn't bear to part with them. I couldn't face the idea of wearing only sarongs and baggy thin pants, as if that would somehow be the last break with my normality, and I'd lose my old self.

★

The day before we left for Banaras I went to the market with Fred. He said he needed some stationery, tape and plastic wrap for making parcels. In the cycle rickshaw on the way, Fred started talking to me about his father. He was born in India, you know, he said. You've kept that one quiet. Nothing more to say about it. The mechanism of the bike clicked as the man in front pedalled and wiped sweat from his brow with an old rag. Emaciated is how I suppose you might describe him now, looking back, that man who pedalled us so slowly because each rotation seemed painful to him. Indian Army kids, two-a-penny in Gloucestershire, he said, the countryside is chocka with people who sailed back and forth by steamship and didn't know their own parents. He told me how his grandfather had hesitated when he met his father at the docks of Bombay because at first he didn't recognise the awkward boy with pimples, standing on the dock after so many years in boarding school, must have fucked him up, he added, and I did wonder afterwards why he was telling me all this out of the blue, when he'd been so reluctant to ever say anything specific about his old man, as we clambered down from the knackered old trishaw.

At the market, I think it was Chandni Chowk, the shops open to the roadside, fat men in white singlets, penned in by their bags of grain, little necklaces of rupee packets of soap powder and detergent hanging down in strips. A cow asleep in an inconvenient place. A man in beige ladling out thick brown tea, and the ladies sitting nearby with spices spread out in front of them, tiny mountains of red and yellow dust. The red spit on the municipal walls and the sudden smell of piss around some corners.

Anyone can tell you these things. Truth be told, these were not the things that interested me. I noticed those details, but what I cared most about that day was Fred. I cared about keeping up with him, watching the way that he moved, the shape of his tanned shoulders under a vest, wondering if he'd look back to hold my hand in the crowd when things got too busy. I felt the burning eyes of all the stallholders and shoppers on us, and the fact that they thought we were a couple. Married? said the man at one cloth shop while Fred was inspecting many soft lengths of silk in rainbow colours. Yes, I said, reaching for my ring instinctively and twisting it hard, yes, he's my husband.

Nice sarees for your wife, sir? said the man, when Fred was at the cash desk, watching his stationery and other purchases being bundled in bags, while another fellow laboured on a long receipt. Yeah, sure said Fred, and he gave me a wink which was so perfect that even those shopkeepers must have thought we were a beautiful match, how well suited we looked, and perhaps some dirtier thoughts crossed their minds, about the way we would look limbs entwined together, and they wished us a long and happy married life. I knew then that Fred couldn't just leave me – the journey couldn't just come to an end – even those shopkeepers could see how we were destined to be together. They would have said it was our karma, but I knew it was up to me to make it happen.

PART 6

FREAK STREET

19

I've come to the days in Banaras now, and I will try and describe them accurately, although it is difficult to recall every detail of that time. It was immediately apparent that Banaras was another ball game, even after all we'd already seen. The drive east was many hours, hard going, and the sky was a different colour once we reached the city, orange, so that the sunsets and the cloth that the pilgrims on the Ganges wore faded into one another, the city all built up as an antique jumble of life and death, the colour of pale flames, on the western side of the banks. The acrid burning smell of that place hit us immediately on arrival.

We found a place overlooking the Ganges, close to the Tulsi Ghat, and that dive we stayed in, well, what should I say? The bed bugs running in a straight line, joining the dots along the line of my back. Amazing how they do that, straight across. As soon as we arrived in Banaras, Fred bumped into a load of freaks that he knew from Kandahar days, some old friends of Chandra, smackheads that Anton had taken against, and that was a worry, and his meditation and yoga unfurled into long silent smoking sessions, glassy eyes, legs crossed on the earth, and Anton and I had a silent compact to keep an eye on him.

Near our hostel on the ghats, all day and all night, burning bodies, bits of bone and carcasses bobbing away. A pall of smoke as heavy as fog, dense with death. Walking along the streets, and then from nowhere a bier would be coming through, face taped up to keep the jaw shut, body shrivelled and precarious, held aloft by the men of the family, tilting, in their bare chests, as close to death as the living could be. And if you followed them, carefully, from a distance, as I did once, you'd see the pyre and the son, with his shaved head, step forwards to poke at the fire, and crack the father's skull, completing his filial duty, the sound of the thwack. And the Ganges, wide and ominous, with froth and petals, and little black boats, licking at the flames, remains of bones like pearls.

Acquiring hash was easy and Freddie had all the best dope from Manali, crumbling it into his palm, eating it neat, sweets from a jar, or baked into brownies by some chick who somehow had access to an oven and offered them out, a sorceress greeting children in a forest. There were rituals he had to complete – handshakes, and smoking in circles, the passing of a chillum. One day he was gone for hours and re-emerged at a shack, a tea place, where he reclined on long floor cushions, generous with his stash, passing on his pipe to whoever was nearby. When he came back the first night, Anton didn't lower his book, pretended he didn't care, never asked what had taken him so long, but he'd look at me and we knew we needed to tread carefully.

He was falling off the wagon again, onto a smorgasbord of substances. You tell him, Anton said, he might take it from you, so I was charged with the conversation. Fred, how about easing up, I said. Huh? On the mind-bending. Oh, Joycie, he looked at me as if I'd suggested something really nasty, and then as if in reply sprinkled out tobacco on the table surface in front of him, crumbling the soft brown strands like compost.

Do you know what? I think you and Anton are too uptight. You can travel the world without seeing the world. It was the kind of thing he said which wound me up, proof that he was taking leave of his senses. I tried a different tactic. We miss you, I said, with heartfelt feeling. Let me tell you a secret, Joyce, he said, and lowered his voice in confidence, every so often I miss myself. I was so frustrated by Fred at that time, so deeply disappointed. That whole trip I had been forming a picture of his future in my mind, had it all planned out for him, could see it plain as day, Fred on the cover of *Rolling Stone* and featured on *Top of the Pops*. Even today when I listen to some of those groups that made it back then, the legends, I think Fred's music would have given them a run for their money. I would still stand by that – his songs had a quality to them. And I imagined him signing with a label and saw the vinyl, and the screaming girls, and Fred at the centre of the stage, demure yet rock solid in the confidence of his voice, lifting his hands up to the crowd, swinging the mike, smiling as they chanted his songs back to him. I wanted that for him, I really did.

Days were losing shape, we were getting up at strange hours, sleeping in the daytimes, up all hours at night;

we had all become unmoored from our homes and our routines and our realities. And we didn't want those things anymore, but we didn't know what we wanted instead. And Fred was undoing himself, shrinking into a thinner, weaker body, hardly ingesting anything except sweet tea and smoke, unburdening himself. He kept giving his belongings away, handing out pieces of clothing, old cassettes, shedding himself of identifying features, trying to dissolve his individuality into the surroundings like sugar into tea. I wanted to hold onto him. I felt as if I was struggling to hold the rope on a hot-air balloon which was straining to lift above the roofs. More than before, he spoke to us in aphorisms and remembered phrases, things he'd picked up from other travellers, sketchy bits of books and prayers, Kahlil Gibran, Rumi, blended with the odd bit of biblical wisdom. He traded herbal remedies with the other freaks for imaginary maladies, little sachets of turmeric and saffron, avoided medicine even when he needed it. Where was his own song? His own music? I hadn't heard him sing for weeks.

Fred wasn't alone; a lot of the westerners couldn't handle Banaras, it was too much, too close to death, there were stories about Englishmen losing the plot there. Mad dogs in the midday sun, unable to handle the sights. People could react badly to it, get strange, aggressive, stupid. Too much death in your face. I think we should move on tomorrow, Anton said. Let's get our shit together. Let's get Fred out of here.

We thought Fred was at a tea place he'd taken a fancy to, off a side street, near the Hanuman Ghat. It took us a while to locate it but when we did, Fred wasn't there. It was still daytime, though a pink moon was out. Someone said he'd headed to the party at Beniya Park.

Was it a party? As we approached the smell on the air was of something holy, like frankincense and the cigarette ends glowed, fire coals. The beautiful bodies of young people naked or nearly naked, topless women in a trance with their hands raised, swinging from hip to hip. The gathering happened without anyone knowing it, without invitations, so nobody knew who was in charge or whose idea it was in the first place. A public park near a derelict shrine; worshippers had left behind yellow marigolds and coconuts. By the time we reached the middle of the crowd the music was blasting out of a battery-powered cassette player which someone had rigged up to a loudspeaker.

The sun was coming down fast and the sky was peppered with flies and mosquitoes. All the feet trampling down the grass as they danced and swayed. A man in a crimson turban went around hugging newcomers and a dog who looked mangy and flea-bitten hobbled from group to group to be petted and loved for a moment. A lot of men were near-naked too, and I remember the dark hair around their nipples and their thongs, and my embarrassment at being so close to so much flesh, and their penises lolling to the side, and the smell of sweat which came from their bodies as they sat in circles with pipes and chillums and bongs, their legs and arms a riot of twisted bracelets and silk strings in rainbow colours. Some of the men and women kissed softly, without intent, as if they were melding into one another.

Anton put his arm around me protectively, for ballast, and we entered the fray and asked people had they seen our friend, Fred, an English guy with blonde hair. Some of them ignored us or shrugged and I realised it was pointless describing Fred to this crowd, that I could hardly recall any of his distinguishing features myself. The earring, the purple trousers – he could have been mistaken for many of them. We approached a group of girls who were weaving flowers in each other's hair. One of them offered me her spliff immediately, without even looking at me, as if she perhaps didn't want it anymore herself. Oh, the English duke? She mumbled in an American accent. Son of an earl actually, said Anton. Whatever. He's here, I've seen him. Another one agreed, her eyes were closed, and she nodded, the boy with the guitar, without giving any more detail.

Come on, Joyce, help me find him, Anton was sober and focused on the task. Anton and I wandered that party for another while, perhaps an hour or more, as it turned to darkness. Some guys tried to start a campfire and the electric music was replaced with singing and harmonies from the girls, and at any moment I thought Fred would be there at the centre of a circle, or lying back with his hands tucked behind his head, admiring the stars. We gave up at about eight o'clock, when it was becoming difficult to distinguish any of the shapes of the bodies dancing around the fire in the shadows and spiralling smoke, and accepted that he wasn't there. Then the American girl came and draped an arm over me, and she gave me an address.

Fred was with a group of full-on freaks. They were slouched in the middle of the lane, in the muck and the dust. Bare feet and wasted eyes. One with a beard down to his chest, a girl who was with him and looked about sixteen. They were taking it in turn to pass a chillum around, and Fred's hands gripped the base of the pipe in supplication, face turned to the sky, Bom Shiva, while he inhaled. And then, after what seemed like minutes, the exhalation of a cloud, the fog wreathing his head.

There was no joy in his circle, it wasn't a party. The others looked like smackheads. A man with a cart of putrid fruit steered around their little circle, another passer-by tutted with disapproval. What the hell, Fred?, you can't do a chillum here, Anton said. You've just watched me, said Fred, and his eyes rolled back into his head a little. What was legal or illegal wasn't the point. The point was we were losing our friend. He was more absent than present. I wanted to share the same consciousness with him, I didn't want him to be on another plane. Looking at Fred then, I realised he was a freak, he was one of them, this wasn't acting. His nails were broken and black with charas, and his eyes no longer focused on my face. His look was detached.

Come on, Anton said, your carriage awaits, and he lifted up Fred's backpack for him, moving towards the van. I need to see some people, Fred said, which was code for needing more dope. He went inside and I followed him inside the dive. Inside it was very dark and I started to make out the shapes. A man was sticking his hand under the shirt of the young girl with plaits, and she was squirming, trying to back away, and two guys had instruments out, some kind of Indian instruments, that they tried to play like snake charmers, so we couldn't hear her protests, and there were lines of Coke bottles, and no one knew whose drink was which, so you could get switched around and end up drinking Johnny Walker and Coke when you just wanted Coke. And the waiters brought things and took things, beckoned on curled fingers, staring if they were young, or looking away straight ahead into the middle distance if they were not. And everywhere, the thick fog of a smoke which was a cocktail of perfume and dope and incense, all messed into one kind of inhalation; you might have got stoned in those places through the water or the air, even if it was never your intention. These kids, who'd been brought up to wash their hands and sit up at the table, and never put their elbows down, and never lick their knife – they were licking all the knives, they were tearing up the rule books, they were dancing around fires, and thinking they were older and wiser, well, that's what they kidded themselves about.

I led Fred outside by the hand. He clambered into the passenger seat, and I put the key in the engine. Anton got in the back and that was when Fred's backpack fell open. It was a mess of scraps of paper and a tobacco pouch and silk scarves, and before he'd gathered the bits from the floor of the van among the shadows, Anton was saying quietly, what are you doing with my dictionary? Fred shrugged. Anton said, very slowly and in a voice I hadn't really heard before, Fred, what have you done to my dictionary? What's wrong with it? Anton was cradling the book, three inches thick, bound in navy leather. The gold writing on the spine and front cover. And then I saw that the spine was out of alignment. And when he tipped open the cover, it was a joke-shop book, a gap where pages should be. I can't believe this. Look what he's done. He showed me the book and, as I feared, it was the one which Sameer had given him back in Iran. Fred had taken a penknife to it, dug out a hollow cube five inches square so that the words were cut in half and the book had a hole just the right size for a generous slab of hash. Anton flicked through the severed pages, the small underlining and pencil notes in the margins of the book. Man, I'll get you another dictionary. Fine bookshops in Delhi. Better than getting busted, laughed Fred. And even worse, more pages were falling out, translucent scraps of pages with hundreds of words on them were scattered all over the floor of the van.

You are a spoilt prick, Freddie. We all sat in the car in silence for a moment. I stared ahead at the windscreen, didn't dare turn the engine on. You're using this country like your playground, like some sort of fairground to hang out in, because it's cheap and because it isn't home so you can get away from your goddamned father. Face up to the earl, darling.

Anton, you are such a bore. What do you really know? Everything you know is out of books. I'm not sure those books are even right anymore. Taking exactly the same photographs, turning them into a backdrop for your own little Kubla Khan fantasy, Mister Anton Sahib. Fucking chump!

Anton got out of the van and shouted, out! He opened the passenger door and started tugging at Fred's arms, hauling his bare skinny arms out from his waistcoat as he pulled. Anton's body had more strength in it, even though he was shorter, and Fred gave off a passive laughing resistance, disbelieving as Anton yanked him out onto the road. We were on a dark roadside, and it wasn't a place to leave a friend. The little circle of oddballs still lolled on the ground, barely concerned. Anton. You can't leave me here. Watch me. Anton climbed up into the seat. Drive, he ordered me. I had been looking dispassionately ahead and I looked down to see Fred sprawled on the yellow road, almost revelling in his debasement, rolling on the ground, laughing out, piss off, Anton. An addict in bare feet. Drive, Anton commanded. And, of course, I did.

In the van, Anton said, I thought this was the trip of a lifetime, but it's all disintegrating. Fred is flipping again. You're out of money. Do you honestly think we'll look back on this now and say it was a blast, Joyce? We will, I said. Are we really going to laugh about Banaras one day? Anton sounded hopeless. But I thought, yes, we will, nobody on the road takes themselves seriously for too long.

That was Anton's failing, he took it all so seriously, as if it was life and death. For the rest of us, death wasn't even in the picture, it was something that belonged to the elderlies back home, with their hats and twinsets. Death was the queen and the post office and settling up with the coalman. It was a metaphor, not something that would actually come knocking for you in the form of a canker or a catastrophe on a dark road. That's what we felt. That's how we all felt. That we would always be completely alive.

20

The next morning I could smell the cremated ashes on the breeze even before I'd opened my eyes. My body itched with the bedbugs and the mosquito bites. I looked up from the bed and Anton was standing at the door of the dormitory with a heavy heart. He needed a witness to what he'd discovered. You've got to come with me, Joyce, he said, and he led me down a dusty staircase to the room he was sharing with Fred on the other side of the building.

The bedspread was patterned with psychedelic flowers, and there was a small shoebox filled with heads of the gods, Shiva, Buddha. These were poor-quality, plaster of Paris things, about five inches tall, padded by Hindi newspapers, but easily smashed or chipped with force. Poor parodies of the carvings that graced the temples. And inside each godhead were packets of white powder, cocaine, little colourful tabs of LSD, larger seed packets of mescalin. And all the equipment for packaging the gear, the little factory tools, spread out like evidence from a crime scene: white glue, razor blades, plastic wrap and cardboard. Anton had found the box under the bed in their shared room. I think, looking back, that he knew what he was looking for, that he'd known for a long time, but that it had taken him this long to see what sat right in front of him, as plain as the nose on his face.

The thing was, in those days, the Indian police let you get on with things if you were smoking for private use. Pharmacies would dole out a little bit of ganja, some of the holy men were off their nuts, there was a fairly easy-going attitude to hashish, even to opium. But making money, shipping parcels out, buying and selling in those kind of quantities, bringing in chemicals, all those repeated trips to the post office, that was a whole other game. That put you in harm's way.

We waited together for Fred to return, sombre as grieving parents, and he came in before long, unslept, humming. He'd hitched back with someone on a motorbike and looked unconcerned, hair a pale tangle. He took in the scene and said, oh, you've found my little godheads. He threw himself down into a chair. I'm not coming to visit you in an Indian prison, Fred, Anton said. There are worse prisons of my own making, he shrugged. The more enraged Anton became, the more languid Fred seemed, singing under his breath, stretching out his legs. He knew just how to push Anton's buttons. I'd never seen Anton so angry – he was raging, all his demeanour crumbled. He couldn't believe that after all we'd been through Fred would continue to put his own life up for auction, and he was scared, scared of all of us getting caught.

Fred was putting us all in harm's way. He was screwing up and taking us down with him. I don't understand, even now, why he couldn't just pull himself together – be a man – focus on making something of himself. Spineless. I wanted to shake him.

Fred tried to make up an excuse. Listen, if I'm not taking a penny from my father, I need to make my own way, right? I need a source of income. I want to be my own person.

I don't know why you've got such a problem with your father now, Anton spat back. We all know he's done far worse things than chasing skirts.

The air blistered. It was a hot day and the electricity was down; the heat in the room was overpowering.

I don't know what you're getting at, but I think you need to be careful, Fred said.

The fan wasn't turning, and the walls were radiating heat.

Come on, don't play the innocent. If you want to talk about your father, then let's talk about Kalari. Get real. Fred's face was disbelief and recognition. Do you have something to say to me, Anton? There was a warning note in Fred's tone, and he shook his head, wilfully sobering up. He stopped fumbling for a beedi and sat up straighter. Anton didn't want to finish his sentence. Bloody events were in the air, things that couldn't be unsaid, that much was clear. I don't know what you're talking about. Come on, spit it out. I want to know what you're saying.

Fred, look, aren't you in the least bit fucking curious? To know the truth?

This made me a right patsy; I hadn't the foggiest what he was talking about and, to be fair to myself, it wasn't as if it had ever been front-page news. In fact, it was, in retrospect, a very minor episode in that historical event. It hardly garnered any attention at the time. Even in thick history books that have been written since, in more recent years. I've looked through these to assure myself of the facts (indeed I borrowed a number of tomes from our local library, and I've made loan requests for the most up-to-date editions written by distinguished historians) and I can promise you that it was only ever a couple of pages, or even just a footnote, even in the specialist books. 'The Kalari incident' it's often called nowadays. Anton was making far too much of it.

The basic facts were simple enough: twenty-three men, taken to a scaffold and hung. Folks from Kalari had been making a great song and dance, taking a petition to an international court, saying it was a deliberate act, ordered from the top. The British rebuttals were always very firm. Entirely regrettable. Entirely blameless. Not something that could be pinned on anyone. Fred's father had been at the top of the pyramid. Entirely exonerated.

But still Anton went on. It was on your father's watch. Why don't you simply ask him about it? So he got the club memberships, the regimental huzzah. Trixie as good as spelled it out to you. Good lord, man, take the blinkers off. You are in so much denial. He's not me, Fred said, defiant as a little boy.

They were hung, Fred. With a noose. Anton made an ugly grasping gesture around his neck with his fingers. They let the floor swing open. Like they did to Cromwell, but in nineteen fucking fifty-three. Chaps younger than us. Down they went, hands behind their backs. Hoods over their eyes.

Stop, I thought, stop now, Anton, but he couldn't help himself. They were the wrong men. They were innocent kids. In the wrong place at the wrong time. Rounded up in the forest. One even had an alibi: he'd been at night school, learning English. Read about it. They came from a completely different village. Have you heard the families talk about the state of the bodies? – before they'd died, they had done things to them. Unspeakable things.

I raced to figure out the right thing to say. And yet why should this matter in the least bit to Fred? Why was Anton bringing it all up now? It was all history, and he wasn't responsible. Surely the greater issue was the drugs in the box? I didn't know why Anton was making such a big deal about something so long ago, I interjected, it's hardly Fred's fault, is it? It all happened when he was so young, I think you're making way too much of this, it's old news. And there was a part of me which felt, though I didn't say it, it all happened in a wild place, like the deserts we'd just rumbled through, where laws worked to a different logic. Just like the place where we sat, not home, not a place where an Englishman with his wife and their little boy could have ever felt safe or known the right thing to do.

Anton couldn't help backtracking. He was kind at heart. He lowered his voice and tried to defuse the situation. Look, I know he was under pressure. It's not so different to what was going on elsewhere, man – I mean, look what the French did in North Africa… and the Dutch in the East Indies… Keep rowing, Anton, I thought. Hard to make the right call, for men on the spot. Anton had gone into his own historical flight of fancy, the events unreeling before his eyes like one of those late-night documentaries: bare-chested men rounded up behind wire, jabbed with the butts of rifles, cabinet members around a table in Downing Street scratching their heads, the gas lamp burning late into the night in a district HQ. It was hot, an insect ran down my sternum in a straight line, only then I realised it wasn't an insect at all but a trickle of sweat.

I think you should keep your fucking oar out of my family, Fred said. You don't know what happened. Nobody does. You weren't there. There's a lot of hearsay, a lot of rumour. There's not a shred of evidence. I thought Fred sounded a little different, as if he was back among the men of his clan again, the slippage into regimental language. Some families have responsibilities, you understand? I guess deep down Fred and Anton had known all this information all along, but it was as if all these horrible old stories were now lit up with floodlights. Anton had been picking up a lot of books in Delhi, and he'd been turning things over in his mind. Look, you know how much I like your dad, he's been first-rate to me, and your mother was—

I was glad that Anton had hit a brick wall. It was my view at the time – and remains so – that Anton was wrong to stick his nose into all that business. Fred's dad was a hero, why was Anton trying to tarnish his medals? Fred swept his boxes of gear and all the packaging equipment to one side and lay down on the bedspread in his clothes, and lolled his arms so they brushed the floor, and yawned and said, Anton, I am so knackered and I don't know what you're talking about, man, will you just fuck off and let me get some sleep?

Those folks in the forest in the 1950s – well, it was all so long ago. I cared so much more about Anton and Fred than about those strangers who swung from a scaffold. Anton thought knowing stuff about the past could magically fix the present. As if he could mend Fred by getting him to confront all that nasty business. I think he should have left well alone. Those folks in Kalari – well, their story wasn't our story, and there's no point pretending otherwise.

Anton took off for Agra the next morning, at dawn, slipping out of the guest house as the pilgrims gathered to bathe on the banks of the Ganges in the rising sun. I heard the rustle under my door, the note saying he'd meet us back in Delhi in a couple of days. He'd be back on Thursday night, he promised, and would meet me for dinner at the Best Exotic Rooftop. He was not going to miss seeing the Taj Mahal. He was heading for the train station and would find a berth on a second-class sleeper if he could get a reservation at such short notice. He was sorry to leave me with Fred. It was time to think about return tickets to England.

Reading that note was painful, like a separation. I felt a deep ache in my gut. I had a hundred questions, and a lot of them were about me, about us, about the journey that lay ahead. What should become of us now? How would we sell the van? Would we take the journey back? And about money – I had very little left, dwindling rupees, and a flight seemed out of the question without some help from the boys now. The truth was that the three of us were braided together, indivisible, we'd been tied into one and we were meant to complete that road together, I was sure that we were all knotted like rope, twisted into one whole and I wasn't going to let Anton just unwind like that.

I'm not going to Agra, Fred said. It's full of tourist tat and scams and pushy men who want to make you buy a carpet. And he's the one who should be apologising, darling, I'm not chasing after Anton like a little kid with pigtails in the playground. We can find him in Delhi, or he can fuck off back to Blighty, frankly I've had enough of his schoolmaster act. I was the one who persuaded Fred, there's no avoiding that fact. This is not a story full of my excuses, you'll have realised by now. We're only a few hours behind him, we'll track him down, I said, ignoring his whingeing. You are coming with me, Fred, and we will find him. We can wait there by the entrance to the Taj and we'll see him appear. There'll only be one gate and we can't miss him. It was a hare-brained plan but there was a certain sort of logic to it. I had realised as I flicked frantically through the rail timetable, a bulging book of tiny digits, that if he boarded the express train the earliest he could get there was six in the morning. We'd get there ahead of him. In my mind I imagined Anton wandering in under the last stars before dawn. The famous dome rising as the moon faded. The boys embracing perhaps in the reflected pearly light. It seemed possible, I wanted to make it happen. There's one road, a national highway, straight as an arrow. Damn dangerous road, that one, said Fred, parroting something he'd picked up from another traveller. We'll do it in twelve hours or so with my foot down. I'll drive, I said. We'll stake out the ticket-office, sit pretty, wait for him. We won't miss him, we will just wait by the gateway. And then you can apologise and we can see this trip out properly. We're sticking together, OK?

You see, all my intentions were good. I made Fred drink hot tea and folded his clothes and put them into the backpack. I boiled up water and added droplets of iodine and filled our bottles. I checked the tyre pressure on the van and made sure we had enough petrol. Fred was in one of his churlish moods, and it was better that I drove because, frankly, he would have been unsafe behind the wheel. He'd been drinking hard liquor – whisky, I think – as well as coming down from something, which made him morose. I couldn't rely on him to drive. He smelled sour and untrustworthy. He was fiddling with little tablets and tincture bottles, as if he had to get the pH balance in his system right.

It was a day of hard driving and I pressed on, barely speaking. We had the windows rolled down and grit and sand and orange dust irritated my eyes, and pieces of straw and sugar cane came off in clouds from the harvest lorries in front of us. I preferred not to drive at night, but I needed to get Fred away from Banaras, away from the death. He hadn't wanted to leave the city and I had threatened and cajoled to get him in the car; I was hell-bent on taking him to Agra, and then, well, I had ideas – fantasies, I suppose you could call them – about us all leaving together, we might sell Vera for more than we expected and get first-class British Airways tickets and drink gins from the hostess trolley and make our way to the grand Palladian house, where we could lounge around and work out what to do with the rest of our lives. We needed to get Fred into a studio and get a record cut – a record deal, that was what he needed.

One of the van's headlamps was blown by that point. The other only gave me ten yards. I was driving quickly, some might say recklessly, determined to find Anton in Agra and then return to Delhi and to get out, I'd had enough. And, aside from my other fine ideas, I guess you could say I wanted to return home and I had, like an onset of illness, a longing for England, and the lidded grey skies, hovering on the horizon gravid with rain, and pulling on a heavy coat, the brisk chill of a winter morning. And Fred worried me. He felt to me like a little flame that I had to keep alive. He was beside me in the passenger seat, looking out into the darkness, little villages interspersed by miles of fields. Fred, I'm going home I said. I've had enough of this performance. But we haven't been to Kathmandu, he protested. I don't give a monkey's about Kathmandu, I said. We've got to see the Himalayas before the monsoon starts. Everyone says so, he whispered. They glow all pink you know, like rose quartz. I think you've got to go home and face the music. Get on with life. This isn't reality, you know, we've been living in this fantasy too long. I'll come with you. I want to...

We were entering a village, there was a small tea kiosk arranged under a single fluorescent light, otherwise hardly visible in the dark. I nearly said I loved him. I thought he would come with me, to be with me, that he understood that I was going to make things right for him, that I believed in his immense talent and that together we would be able to turn his talent into something eternal; his songs would be played by young couples at their weddings or chanted in unison in stadiums, songs that would be requested on radio shows, his music would live on. So, should we go back to the Clapham House first, do you think, Fred? I'm not coming with you, go back if you want to, he responded. I ignored him. I think we should leave next week. It shouldn't be too hard to book the tickets. But he was determined. England's over for me, this is my life here now. I'm staying here. Tears welled in my eyes. That can't be true. I'm through with England, Joyce, I'm on a different path. Fred, I've got a plan, I know what to do, I'm right. You have to believe that I'm right. I can't believe you're throwing everything down the drain. You're not listening, Joyce. I've said it so many times. It's over. And that was when I accelerated in blind fury.

At the roadside, near the kiosk, some local men were sipping hot tea, relaxing on charpoys, putting the world to rights. Muhammad Bakshi, the young chaiwallah, later the leading witness, saw a van – a dirty green Land Rover – overtaking a public bus on the Agra Road, beeping its horn repeatedly, furiously – and an oncoming truck in the other direction, the bus driver turning sharply on instinct. He ran out with arms raised towards the road in dismay. Frantic, hopeless in a village forty miles from a hospital, with one telephone line.

And the vehicle – the death van, the newspapers called it – didn't stop; it swerved and disappeared around the corner, Bakshi waiting for it to turn back in conscience and realising that it had vanished into the dark night of sugarcane fields. The glint of death in the truck driver's eye. A ball of flame. The world burst. I saw it happen in the rear-view mirror as I veered back onto the left-hand side, the bus swerving, and the sickening crunch as it rolled over into the ditch. We wavered for a sorry moment. The truck became smaller as we raced away, disappearing like a firework on the horizon. And then there was no bus in front of us and no bus behind us.

Keep driving, Fred whispered, just keep driving, OK. I should turn back, I said, as I pressed the accelerator. Keep going, Fred said, pale and ghostly beside me. The fields were black on either side, fields of something strange and unknown to us. The night before us, and all that had happened was a black hole that had sucked light from the sky. We drove for many miles. Pull over, said Fred, and I did as he said. We sat there by the side of the road, the frightening sounds of insects in the fields around us. Fred pulled out a cigarette and lit it, handed it to me. He took another for himself. As I held it I saw that it trembled in my hand.

Listen, my old fruit, I was driving, OK? If anyone comes for us, it was me behind the wheel. We're going to change places now. They might not find us. I had a ridiculous surge of hope. What's meant to be will be. I can't let you, Fred, your future... I have my father, he interjected ruefully. And even as I got out and walked around to the passenger seat it was impossible to connect the words with that firework.

Then we saw the road sign, lit by our one headlight, that announced we were only ten miles away from Agra, and in our confusion and fear we stuck to the original plan and drove slowly into the outskirts of Agra, where we sat shaking for a long time in the front seats in a poor alleyway with an open gutter, waiting for the sun to rise again, and I longed to wake from this fever dream, or for a pill that would wipe my memory, and I ached to see Anton more than ever. When the darkness was sliding away, we pulled a tarpaulin over the van and left it under a large banyan tree.

We didn't speak. Like automatons, we found a rickshaw, which weaved through the streets. Fred handed over hundreds of rupees, just emptied out his pockets, and I knew when we'd reached the Taj Mahal because of a gate and a wall and the crowds and Fred telling me to get out. And we crouched like fugitives in the shadows of the ticket-office, and that was when the waiting started. Two ticket sellers sat side by side in a booth, issuing receipts with patience through a grille. Little green stubs. The foreigners' price was ten times the price for the locals and the Indians passed through the turnstile lightly, going for a picnic, large families together, schoolgirls with immaculate plaits holding hands in crocodiles. The foreigners with more reverence and more cameras, often alone. We were on the outside, under the shade of a tree. I watched every single man that morning who passed through the gateway, heading towards the swollen dome. None of them were Anton. I remembered what Big Red had said about trying to spot tigers in Corbett National Park; they'd been there for three days and, in the end, every single thing was a tiger, every shadow between leaves, every movement in the grass. They never saw one. I understood that as the sun bore down on us: a man with glasses turned and I saw an aspect of Anton's face, a guy swept his hands through his dark hair and I jumped up, ready to run to him. Every time I was wrong. I wondered if he'd passed when I blinked or if he'd slipped behind a crowd, if there was another entrance.

Fred, will you bloody well keep your eyes open? He'd sunk down onto his backpack, using it as a pillow, and his eyes looked bloodshot, barely capable of searching. I didn't trust him to keep guard, but I needed to sleep too. My eyes sagged and I rested my head on his shoulder. I might have slept for an hour or more. My jaw was slack heavy when I woke and the sun had moved into our corner so we were under the rays, and my hair felt burning to the touch. Joyce, he said gently. He's not here. I think we should go now. This is getting weird. I told myself: maybe the train was delayed, or cancelled, or he changed his mind. The sun was pressing on my skull, red hot and relentless. The ticket sellers remained the same all day, and one of them looked at me pityingly from his booth. A couple of bums, without the money to get inside the Taj.

Just a bit longer, I pleaded. Fred agreed to stay until sunset. I watched the line more intensely, repeatedly standing and walking up and down, studying the faces. The weathered freaks, the smart pilgrims. All strangers. So many thousands of strangers. A feeling of dread had started to swell in my body, although I'd have been hard-pushed to say where it was located. In my belly, I told myself, dodgy water. Shock and tiredness. It was easy to explain. We were safe, OK, there had been an accident, we hadn't collided with anything. Everyone knew what happened if you pulled over. The way that village justice was served. It was easy to make excuses, and under the sun it was hard to know what was real anymore, what might have been a dream in a van. Fred hadn't said a lot, he had retreated inside himself. His silence was troubling me. One tourist had the same bag as Anton, the same army surplus. I ran up to him, and then retreated, sorry, my mistake, I mumbled. I looked at the sky and asked for a sign or a symbol. There was no reply. Fred insisted: Joyce, we are going now. Come on.

We drove away as the sun came rolling down over the Taj Mahal. The dome was a luminous pearl as we headed in the wrong direction, turning our backs on that view. The monument to love in the rear-view mirror was the saddest thing I ever saw.

21

We returned to Delhi in the middle of the night and a drowsy watchman sleeping on a rush mat on the floor let us in when we banged on the hostel door. We crept in like thieves and turned away from each other on the first-floor landing; I was going towards the women's dormitory and Fred towards the men's. Fred caught me and squeezed my hand as we parted. I still felt the grit from the road in my eyes and thought I could smell burning. Perhaps it was woodsmoke. I don't remember collapsing into bed that night, and I think I slept, and when I awoke it was with the full and terrible realisation of what had happened the previous night, the total disbelief that anything like that could have ever taken place. There was birdsong straining above the Delhi traffic and one of the girls in the dormitory was brushing her teeth using a mug to spit into, and there was a faint refrain of a Bollywood melody coming from a radio on a balcony. Nothing on fire, nobody had clamped me with handcuffs. The day looked like any other day on the road. The bus was a *trompe l'oeil*. The crash was a state of mind.

Anton had said he'd meet me for dinner on the roof terrace that Thursday night when he returned. But he didn't come. I washed my clothes in the sink with a bar of hard green soap, ate a banana pancake at the Rooftop. The next night he still wasn't back. My clothes were stiff from the sun and I folded them all into tight squares and repacked my bags.

I couldn't sleep all night for the car horns going incessantly, and a gecko on my wall with its sudden disappearances, and the heat which created delirium even when I wasn't sick. Dreams of endless caves and roads without end. I woke early feeling that I needed to find Anton, to warn him of something. A feeling of dread which was soaking my skin like sweat. Crossing to the dormitory I could see that his bed was empty, that he still hadn't returned. Let him have some playtime, Fred would have said. I was used to Fred coming and going. With Anton it was different – I trusted him, we kept to a timetable, held agreements. Another day passed, it was Sunday and still no sign of Anton.

Where the hell is he? I asked angrily. I knew he'd been mad with Freddie but I never thought it would come to this. Not abandonment. Surely not. Without a word? It wasn't Anton's style. We've got to look for him, I said to Fred, waking him up, shaking him. His legs lolled off the bed. He can't just vanish. Maybe some bad people. I didn't want to think of the dark places that Anton went late at night. Two words, needle and haystack, Fred mumbled, still with his eyes closed. Fred, I was physically shaking him now, I'm scared. When I shook his legs they seemed so slight, so lacking in muscle or bone, as if he might just slip away too. They couldn't both leave me. Anton is out there in this city and we've got to find him. Vera sat outside accusingly. There was no one propelling us onwards. It seemed in the silence of the engine that our journey had come to an end. Where should I look? Hospitals? Embassies? Maybe you'll think I was daft but I headed to the National Museum. Even if it wasn't the place I thought Anton would be, it was where I thought he would want to be if he could choose.

A ghost zone. Cabinets put in place by the Victorians, the wood all the same universal colour, hinges and the smell of mothballs and creosote. I looked through the glass panes and they looked back at me: dead kings with flat faces, and tiny little coins which told stories of battles lost, forts conceded, and then rows of cannonballs – sanitised, cleaned, of blood and hair and dirt. How to make sense of it all without Anton? What would we do without him? The panic was rising in me, in the long corridors where occasionally another visitor would slip into view and then vanish again. I could see Anton in the glass panes, in reflections, in the shadows of others; I had to get out of that place.

Then I walked some more. Moving on and off the pavements set high above the ground, lined with yellow. Warning stripes. I walked back to the hostel, and near the place where the road turned from the railway colony into Paharganj there was a dog with three legs, limping, and it kept looking at me, and then limping alongside me, as if it wanted to tell me something. I must have been looking hard at that dog, staring, and probably standing still in the street, because a young man who looked like he was on the way to the office, with slicked back hair, pens in his pocket and a purposeful walk, said road traffic accident, madam, trying to explain that dog to me, and it was then that I knew. It was as simple as that.

Fred was waiting for me in the guest house lobby and he was sitting in a chair, upright. Hands clasped together. Calm and officious, as sober as a judge. There's been an accident, he said. My mind moved forward, efficiently, to hospital visits, taking grapes, arranging the best care, letting his mother know. I might have even pictured him with a drip, into his long brown arms. Joycie. The bus – head on – overturned. I was with a living Anton for a fraction longer, determined to stay with him for one more second. Joycie, you aren't listening. He's dead.

A sweeper who usually cleaned the toilets had already been to the roadside to wash off the blood, crouched down on his haunches, swiping at the ground with a firm brush. The room was full of people, picking up his things, one policeman turned over the sheets as if he might find something useful inside the bed. I looked at the inspector's keen, pliant face with his notebook open. Pencil at the ready.

The bus driver had been killed outright alongside three other passengers, and it wouldn't have even been a notable accident but for the foreigner on board, wearing kurta pajamas, who had been trying to speak Hindustani with other passengers. Most firangi took a tourist bus, air-conditioned, the policeman said, perhaps in kindness, perhaps in judgement. He stood with his hands on his hips and I remember his wide brown leather belt. Fragments of the crash came to us. It was on the inside pages of the local press, a completely unremarkable road traffic accident. The truck driver said the bus had swerved to avoid a van, hard and very fast in front of him, and he'd tried to apply the brakes, and reached for his horn, honking, but the bus had spun, it had danced, he said, trying to find the right English word in front of the police. Lights had been blazing on his truck, it was carrying watermelons from Punjab, there was filmi music playing in the cabin on a tape deck. HORN PLEASE. And in Anton's bus, also, music which carried on, loudly, even when the engine had been crushed and the bus had rolled over and all those people were a confusion of blood and broken skull and splinters of glass.

And Anton, who was sitting on the left-hand side, the better to see the views, I guessed, was on the side that the bus rolled onto, concertinaed, the sound of a metal can crumpled in a fist. Thrown forwards and then down, his head smashed with full force against the window, and his face such a mess that the policemen were terribly embarrassed and moved from one foot to the other, because they didn't want us to look at him but they had paperwork to complete, and there were rules, especially in the identification of foreigners. I'll call his mother, Fred said to the sub-inspector who had been sent out to Paharganj.

Did he get to see it? I said. What? Fred looked blank, hopeless. The Taj Mahal. Was he on the way there or the way back? The way there, said Fred, he never reached Agra, and he didn't seem to care either way, but to me it mattered a lot. The road had broken. We were coming apart at the seams.

It had happened on the Grand Trunk Road. He'd had a passport in his bag, and eventually someone had found it, amid the wreckage, and they'd managed to alert the embassy. The second-class tickets on the express all sold out; he'd been seen by another backpacker, walking away from the train station, debating whether to squeeze into a third-class carriage, whether to curl up on a luggage rack suspended from the ceiling, then eventually changing his plans and opting instead for a clapped-out passenger bus that stopped at every forgettable dusty town instead. Nobody had joined the dots – I could barely join them myself. Nobody had come asking about us, or our whereabouts that night, or the ownership of the faded van. We were the objects of sympathy. It was possible to blank out those seconds on the road, for it all to be nothing more than a simple tragedy.

I found myself crouching on the roadside, sieving dust and stones through my fingers. Come on Joyce, come and play pool, pleaded someone, perhaps Big Red, I know he bought me a lime soda in Connaught Place and tried to talk to me about grief.

I couldn't make sense of the fact that the bodies in the street, Indian bodies of coolies and sweepers, malnourished, sometimes missing limbs, the kid on a platform made from a wooden pallet fixed with wheels which he paddled with his hands, his shrivelled little thigh stumps, how all these fragile bodies could live while Anton was gone. I've never been able to figure it out to this day. How he was outlived by a struggling pot plant in the lobby of the Paharganj guest house, outlived by every single living thing around me in that vast, incomprehensible country.

Watching Fred was the worst part, as he didn't say much at all. For days we circled each other in our own little orbits of grief, noticing how each other had been peeled raw, joined by the shared terror of the Agra Road.

Did we think about going to the embassy or the police? Not for a moment. The story was written. There was nothing we could do or say, and I somehow believed – perhaps Fred did too – that his golden sheen would save us, that he couldn't be touched because he glistened the way that he did, that, like a fairy tale prince he could transform himself into another creature, slip from the clutches of the past, the reach of the law. The Indians call them djinns – the creatures who shapeshift and play with humans, and slip in and out of the mortal world, scurrying off as lizards or scorpions. It was our karma, he said, when I tried to raise it, we would face what happened next, but I wasn't to say anything to anyone. Fred never said another word to me about what happened on the road that night and I feel now, looking back, that I pushed him away, because those were days when the veil between us was thinner than it had ever been, when we could have merged together, I could have even let him caress me and hold me in the darkness. We were bound together by our secret. We should have wept together.

22

We didn't talk much about home or what we'd left behind, as a rule. Some of it wasn't worth talking of – who wanted English bread or to think of drizzle? But there were other things, parents, childhoods, old flames, that people had packed away with their backpacks. The whole reason for being there was to go forwards, I suppose. But now Anton's mother was going to arrive on Thursday, flying into New Delhi, and this gave everything a hard crunch of reality. It should have been Anton's death which woke us up, but it was the imminent prospect of his mother, who I knew so little about, that made me shake with fear. What should we expect? I asked Fred, who had at least met her on several occasions, and he barely answered me, but shrugged.

You are very dear friends. He wrote to us about you. I heard all about your friendship, he wrote to us about your vehicle and the places you have been. His mother had on very large Jackie O sunglasses, which looked quite fetching but I was under no illusions, they were there to hide the black pits of her eye sockets, made puffy and sore with days of crying. We had gone to Palam International airport to meet them, the chap from the high commission gave us a lift to Block 1A in his stately, air-conditioned Ambassador with diplomatic numberplates and flag bouncing on the front bonnet. There may have even been a rotating light on the roof, but I can't recall now.

Anton's mother was tentative with Fred, I could sense that, shaking his hand rather than embracing him, and Fred hadn't done anything to smarten up for the occasion, so I was at once aware of how lithe and peculiar we seemed to her, in our stringy clothes, and with our incense smell, as she walked into the arrival hall in a prim skirt and cardigan, the sort of clothes that made me realise how far I was from English women and their hats. She clutched a leather suitcase, which had been wrapped with black tape like mourning bands. Her hair was permed, you could have seen her shopping on any English high street. How far we had come without ever thinking of these people we had left behind, so that Anton's mother was all of our mothers, all of the prim and rotund women of England, all of the motherliness of the country that we'd run from. It was overwhelming.

The high commission man had arranged an anteroom to the side of the airport arrivals lounge, which was, I thought, a sad room, windowless, vacated for some minutes by a Sikh who had left his desk fan running and scattered papers all over his desk, which I feared would fly away in the draft, the usual overstuffed files bundled to one side. There were hard plastic seats, but we all stood.

She concentrated on me, to my shame, and asked what we had been up to the night before he died, what he had eaten at the hostel, how he had seemed. A lot of complicated and probing questions, all in her downturned voice, with the sunglasses still shading her face from us, not an interrogation but a need; any information that she could backdate, reinsert into the storyline that he had woven and then dramatically shredded. She cried constantly, lines of tears rolling from under the glasses, so that it was hard to imagine her without tears or without dark glasses after some time. And you two were close, I know that. I also saw now that she avoided Freddie completely, and had turned to me in every way, as if there was still a hope there. His normalcy. Even in his senseless, horrifying death, she wanted to be reassured of his normalcy. I could have hurt her then. It would have been easy. But I chose to leave things alone. She knew that we had sometimes shared a room. Let her think whatever she wanted.

But Fred was pacing, looking at her, trying to draw attention to himself. It was possible that she blamed him for what had happened, and in one sense she wouldn't have been wrong – it was Fred who had bankrolled the trip, Fred who had been the accomplice and co-conspirator in the plan to drive the overland. But we all knew that travel was Anton's passion, she knew better than us how Anton had sat with an atlas on his lap as a cross-legged boy, and connected cities with pencil lines and geometry sets, working out the ways in which the world might be crossed. She knew his dictionaries and his habit of learning oriental alphabets even as a child, in order to impress other boys, with the way that he could write their names on their school books in Arabic swirls, right to left. She knew her son, and she knew how he had died, and nothing we could say was going to make it any better.

The high commission man had meanwhile taken the office chair, while we all continued to stand, and looked as if he wished he could vanish, genie-like, to disappear from the scene. But eventually he stirred himself and coughed, and said, our driver is outside, and I think it would be better if we could say farewell to Anton's friends now, and take our leave, Mrs Aziz. Perhaps he had to do this sort of thing every week, perhaps it was part of being third secretary in the Delhi embassy.

They were going to go to the morgue to look at Anton's body. I didn't want to think beyond that fact, if she would want to see it with all the injuries and horrors wrought on it, if they might have been able to make him look peaceful enough for a mother's kiss. The visit had to be arranged quite carefully because there was still press interest in the story and the fear was that there would be photographers lurking for a shot of Mrs Aziz, although in the end that was unwarranted, as no murderer had been found and the story lacked the salacious or criminal undertones needed to attract the western press – Anton was not a beautiful woman for starters – and once it had passed from the inside of the Delhi rags, it faded away, one of the lesser exalted and exotic overseas deaths, one which would take less police time, and be put down to the evil forces which necessarily lurked outside England, which every traveller was risking if they stepped aboard a boat or plane, and, most particularly, an overland bus.

While Mrs Aziz went to the morgue, we returned to the hostel. Freddie had got so thin by this stage that his old clothes looked clownish, excessive. And now he was a sad Pierrot, chin to the floor, a roll-up in his hand but burning out, unsmoked, or unlit. Some other guests at the hostel had heard what had happened, and a couple of them patted Fred on the shoulder as we arrived back in the lobby. Sorry, man, so sorry, but they exited quickly, didn't linger, and I didn't blame them. Ours was the ultimate downer. And we weren't telling the story very well, avoided going into details, there wasn't much to be repeated or exaggerated about the whole sorry tale. It was a smash, he was dead. Other travellers must have found us very depressing to be around.

You want to get a drink? said Fred, we could go across to one of the roof terraces? We sat in silence, nursing brown bottles of beer. The Jama Masjid call to prayer was loud, insistent. We both knew without admitting it that we should leave the country as soon as possible. I'm not going back, said Fred, just as I was thinking these thoughts, and he said the words with sudden vehemence.

Neither of us talked about Anton, but he may as well have been at the table. I thought about how he had wanted to go to university, his ambitions to become a professor. Perhaps it wasn't far-fetched to imagine him living quietly with a handsome man in a central London flat. I see them sitting together in the evening, in a room filled high with books, hand-knotted carpets spread across the floorboards. Or walking around naked whenever they wanted.

Have you told your father? He was fond of Anton, wasn't he? I realised perhaps once more that I was picking at something better left, that this was the wrong thing to say to Freddie at this time. And yet I couldn't stop myself.

Even on this, the worst day, Anton's day, Freddie was the object of my fascination. Joyce, my, my, quite the voyeur as ever. What's in it for you? My face must have shown everything. Oh, Joyce, I'm sorry. I shouldn't have said it. I didn't mean it. I loved his immediate contrition, and his hand in my hand across the table, squeezing.

I can't help thinking, he said, that the gods took the wrong chap. He'd have been better off with Anton as a son. The letters. He told me a little bit about the letters, then. Not everything. There was correspondence between his mother and Trixie, run-of-the-mill notes, but there were also a few letters he didn't expect to find in there, letters between his father and Trixie. I should have showed these to Anton. The Boff knew what he was talking about. He moved his beer bottle aside and took them out of his bag.

Trixie had wanted to know he was safe. The news came in small pieces, cut-up passages of information, the rising price of guns, the way the tribes were gathering, pulled together like iron filings, dispersing, bringing their strange, undecipherable threats. A bomb had gone off, there were body parts on a road. A road he might have driven down. She wrote, hiding everything, hiding feeling, because she thought she must be brave, not to add to his worries, and it was a presumption to think that her feelings mattered. She had no right to fear for him. The conference to settle a new constitution had been postponed already, the stakes had risen to new heights, and in the midst of it was his upright body, trying to do good. Trying to knock their heads together.

We must stay here another six months, I fear, and see the damn thing through, his father had said. Don't go anywhere too dangerous, Trixie had requested. I won't. I promise, he'd replied. And then it had come to head, a tipping point. The final letters were about his return home. Her joy at his return. He handed me the papers. Read them.

Trixie's handwriting was elegant, beautiful cursive slants, everything about the letters was graceful: the creamy paper, in one envelope even a small violet, a pressed wildflower which she had gathered from his own woodlands. And in response the hurried letters from the earl, sometimes typed, sometimes handwritten, but always signed with his love to his darling, his dearest, giving the game away. They burned for each other.

And your mother was still alive, at that time? He sighed. It wasn't exactly a shock, he said, I think I always knew, deep down. I was angry with him. My mother probably knew. But why give them to me? That's what I keep wondering. Why hand them over? He knew the answer to his own question. Fred picked at the label on his empty beer bottle with his nails.

I watched a kite spread its wings, circle and swoop. She wanted to get rid of anything incriminating, anything that linked her to Kalari. He peeled off the remnants of the beer wrapper. No blood on those dainty little hands. Things which had been better kept out of the country and out of the official files. His father's fingerprints all over them. The risk of Britons being killed in some numbers. The probability of facts, a deterrent needed. It was an order. The necessary appearance of legality. One of them was just a kid, a houseboy. And he thought he was doing it for her. He wrote to her about it. He needed to show who was boss, and to stop this thing spiralling in the countryside;

the more he went about in his jeep from place to place, the more the leaks kept springing, like trying to put your finger in the dyke, like the little Dutch boy, that's the way he describes himself in the letters. And the local police were angry, and they had ways of getting information out of people, leaching out confessions. And they needed swift action, and they wanted to send out a message. Trixie said that he'd done the right thing, that he'd done his duty. That he was making the world safer.

I could have understood Freddie breaking at Anton's death. At his father's betrayal. But returning to that old story, long-dead people, something he played no part in, I couldn't understand it. It was, I guess, so typical of Fred, though, to feel the sharp pain of other people that he had nothing to do with and yet struggle to show love for those he needed most. What does all this matter, when compared with Anton's death? I demanded. Talk to me about the present, Fred, about Anton! I can't believe you're wasting yourself on this. You've been torturing yourself about all of this that happened so long ago? You're a brilliant musician and you're so gorgeous. You can do anything. And if it all goes wrong, you can be back in front of the fireplace with the hounds at your feet in no time. It's OK that your old man was a shit. Of course he was a shit! But it was his job. He was a man of his time. Hardly any people died! Just a load of terrorists in a jungle. Talk to me about Anton – about the present, what's happened this week. What the hell do you expect me to say about things that happened decades ago? Did you think I'd kiss it better?

I thought you'd understand, he said, I honestly thought

you would understand. And his face hardened as he looked at me as if seeing me for the first time.

I saw Mrs Aziz one more time after that. She came to collect Anton's rucksack from the hostel the following day. She was in the men's dormitory, the others had cleared out in anticipation, and she stood in the grey light, the fans whirring above her head, lost.

The Indian people have been very kind, she said, and she looked around as if everything was a mystery, nothing made sense in this place; the plug sockets, the sound of horns, the small children who followed her down every street. Over time she might begin to appreciate Anton's beautiful diary, I thought, and his photographs, and his dictionaries but as she laid them all out side by side on the bedspread, she was bewildered by them.

He slept here? she asked, her boy in this bed, among friends, among strangers. She had shed the cardigan, so her bare arms showed, portly and white, an inoculation scar ugly on her upper arm, and I felt a new wave of sympathy for her, and stood closer to her. In his money belt, tucked in a side pocket, was a thick wedge of rupees, neatly stacked in a leather wallet, and another sheaf of uncashed traveller's cheques. I remembered Anton's frugality and felt sorry. Take it, she said, offering it all. I don't need it, I don't want it. I doubted she even knew the value of the notes. I can't. In which case I'll put it in the dustbin with these things. Free to a good home. She indicated the dictionaries and a pile of sketchbooks, along with pants, socks, folded kurtas, worn-out leather chappals, cylinders of undeveloped camera film. She had taken the solid things, the things he had brought with him: the penknife and the camera. The things made in England. I thought she had selected the wrong items but I didn't say a word.

I took the notes, and she looked grateful. To have offloaded some of this flotsam, she wanted her boy home, to seal the old memories, not to pollute them with all this strange foreign junk.

The body was flown back, I think. There must have been a funeral.

At dusk there was a phone call to the yellow ISD booth next to the hostel. Fred was called – summoned: international call, sir – with urgent voices, everyone understanding all too well the rupees burning, the time slipping away on the line, the cost to this unseen caller. But Fred flapped the boys from the ISD booth and the reception away. He sat in the lobby area with a cigarette in his hand, stubborn as a mule, and said, not here, I'm not here. It was clear the caller was not being deterred, that they were hanging on the line, and this was awkward for the telephone booth man who didn't know what to do and didn't want to put down the receiver, and there was a little fuss and exasperation in the lobby.

Here was my chance, I felt sure it must be him, who else would be calling internationally to this hostel? And I felt a little surge of adrenaline and then was sorry that I couldn't share this moment with Anton, who would have enjoyed the details. I'll speak to him, I said, and strode up to the booth. The receiver was warm from the hand of the man on reception who had been holding it up and it felt sticky in my hands. I knew before I heard his voice, the click on the line and the slight buzz – international subscriber dialling – it must be morning there in England, he would have taken breakfast at the long dining table, soldiers and boiled eggs, and considered what to say, he would have spooled the dial with his forefinger, perhaps he was wearing a cravat, a cashmere sweater, standing upright in his study...

Hello. Frederick? A man's voice, deep and filled with authority. I'm sorry, no, my name is Joyce, I'm one of the friends that Frederick has been travelling with, I'm afraid Fred is... unable to come to the telephone right now – but I thought I might be able to help. Ah, yes, Joyce, there was no disguising the fact that he didn't really know much about me, that there was a vague familiarity with my name, little else to go on. I'm a good friend of Fred's, I offered, I thought he should really have known who I was by now. Actually, we've been together since the start, since leaving your house in Clapham, we're very close. Yes, well, I'm calling about Anton. I heard from his mother, Mrs Aziz. I am so terribly shocked and saddened by the news. I wanted to – he seemed genuinely to catch with emotion in his throat – to express that to Frederick. It's been a very difficult time, very difficult, I emphasised. I hoped my voice was conveying my grief too, and the horrors we'd all been through. I heard myself becoming loftier as I spoke to him, raising myself up to his level. The road was busy with evening traffic, and he must have heard the noise of the horns and dogs and motorbike engines revving on my side of the line. I could hear the quietness of England on his side, perhaps even the crackle of a winter fireplace, the room he spoke from was hushed and full of drapery, thick carpets. I could imagine where he stood, in his study, from Anton's descriptions, with a view over the lake. It's been such a shock for everyone. Is there anything I can do? Is Frederick alright? He's alright, thank you. A fat lot of good you can do from there, I wanted to say, with your mess of a son, but I restrained myself. I wanted him to know that I'd done everything I possibly could have done for Fred. I'm taking good care of him, I said. Well, look, if he needs something – if he needs money, perhaps, to return home, will you call me? You have my number? I know people in the Foreign Office. I can help. Yes, we met your friends in Tehran, Trixie and Guy. I said the words heavily, with intent. Trixie sent you her love. Ah, yes, fine people.

There was so much I wanted to say to this man and to ask, but my voice had a stilted formality, reflecting his tone, and the man at the ISD booth was looking at me, watching the dials turning, which counted the seconds and minutes. Fred doesn't want to talk to you at the moment, I'm sorry, I said, but I promise to bring him back to Gloucestershire. I'll accompany him. I guess, as I spoke the words, I had even fooled myself. I've heard so much about the house, I said brightly, about the stucco you've discovered. I thought the least he could do was extend an invitation to me, given all that I'd done, but he ignored my comment. I know that Frederick isn't very pleased with me at the moment. Nonetheless... he trailed off in a genuine sort of bewilderment, I'd be obliged.

23

In the morning, I entered the first place I saw with the words TRAVEL AGENT pasted in the window, and a young Kashmiri guy who claimed to have married a German woman, although she wasn't in evidence, was smoking behind the desk. There was a power cut, he was sitting in the gloom with a stilled fan, faded posters on the walls for unlikely destinations.

American Express was not his preference, but he'd take the traveller's cheques, if he could take them all. He wanted to help me. I ended up telling him about Anton, it sounded like a plea, the way that I told it. He looked pitifully at me. He had ways of cashing them. I'd get a one-way ticket to London in return. It was a standby ticket, a day or two, the airline always had a spare seat, I wasn't to worry.

That night I was sitting with Fred on the rooftop, looking down on the cycle rickshaws and the street hawkers with carts from above. Kites circled above us, looking for scraps of meat, for carrion. The electricity cables and telephone cables strung from the roof, densely matted like witches' hair. I spoke to your father yesterday. Uh-huh. I know. He sounded like a good man, he sounded decent. He wants to help you. Yes, well, he knows the right things to say. What you told me about your father, I started (I had given some thought to what I wanted to clearly point out), Anton did get his facts wrong from time to time. He wasn't *always* right, you know. You can take his version with a pinch of salt.

His face was pained. Actually, Joyce, I don't think you know a single thing about my family. I was stunned. Did he think I wouldn't remember our conversation? Or was he really so drug-addled that things of momentous importance could slip through his speech, as easily as inanities, so that he might not remember what he had said? Your father doesn't sound like the type to carry out those hangings! I said the words cheerily, so he'd understand how much I trusted his family, and how ridiculous all those rumours sounded. Oh, all that carve-up, just forget it, old girl. I'm over it. It's all fine. Just dandy. He picked up a small stone in his fingers and examined it without real curiosity. He turned away from the city view.

I'm heading home, I said, I mean to England. I waited for him to say he was coming home too. I had planned the route from Heathrow back to Gloucestershire. I was fairly sure that Clive wouldn't mind collecting us, and that he'd drive us back to Fred's place – or perhaps we should start off in the Clapham house for a few days, find our feet and spend a couple of days by ourselves in London before going out to the country.

I'm going to clean my act up a bit, my old fruit. Head up to the mountains. Start taking care. Try out some more yoga... surya namaskar and all that, he dangled his arms down to his shins in a loose-limbed way. Gurus in the hills. Fred started coming out with all kinds of claptrap again; that there were men up there over a hundred and fifty years old, you might go for a few days and stay in the caves for years. Transcendental meditation. There were no shortcuts, he was going to do it the hard way. He wanted to learn from a guru. I'd seen them on roadsides, in saffron with leathery feet and begging bowls, sadhus – they frightened me, those men shaking off attachments to the world. Fred's hair had worked itself into matted tendrils since he'd stopped brushing it.

I've bought a plane ticket, I said. It was as if he hadn't heard me. Got to get up to Kathmandu, he said, I want to see those pink lights on the mountains – did you know they look like rose quartz? I said a couple more times, it would be worth getting out, Fred. It was as if the effort of the past days had finished him off and drained his remaining energy. He could have booked a ticket out the next day, there was nothing holding him there. He could have flown out. He had a credit card, after all. It was almost as if he was waiting for the knock. But he made no effort to arrange a ticket, didn't try and get up to Nepal.

I stayed in Paharganj for a few more days. I lose count, to be honest, it's all very unclear to me. All our roads had come to roadblocks, all the routes and maps had lost their ability to direct us or show us a way forward. I saw the Irish lads again a few times, they shook our hands solemnly, said nice words about Anton. There were some days of listlessly playing pool with them, playing to lose, beers in hand. The hostel owner tried to be kind but we were tainted now, living proof that the trail could go bad. We had brought the police to the place. Anton had bad karma. I could tell he wanted us moved on. The Irish lads were waiting for tickets for an onwards sleeper train, second-class AC, which took them away from Delhi early one morning, unexpectedly, without saying goodbye.

The hostel was filled with faces I didn't recognise. Vera sat outside with kids perched on her bonnet, and a child traced a finger through the brown dust which had accumulated on her rear window, to make a smiley face.

The Kashmiri travel agent was as good as his word, and had the aeroplane ticket ready for me, sealed in a cardboard wallet. He handed it across ceremoniously and it became apparent, as we talked, and he retacked one of the corners of the posters showing the crumpled sights of Australia to the wall, that the German woman had gone. She had left him and taken their daughter too, back to the Black Forest. We commiserated with each other, shook hands with heartfelt blessings.

It was a Sunday morning in December, just as the weak, pink Delhi sun was rising, when the taxi arrived to take me to the airport. So we're going to split, then? I didn't want to leave. I lingered some time longer while the taxi driver left the car and went to talk with a huddle of other drivers, as if we had all the time in the world. What will you do? We were holding each other's hands like lovers. He carried my backpack down the stairs for me. I realised that I didn't want a single thing in it. I'd have gladly left it there. I'm going to live in the moment, that's the right thing to do, isn't it? he said brightly. There's a lot of freaks seeking the light up in the Himalayas… that's the place to be. Goodbye, Fred. Goodbye, my dear heart. He smiled at me with his hair catching golden in the dawn and I remembered the first time I saw him, and all the times I'd seen him since, singing his heart out to the world. And perhaps at that moment I should have stayed to watch the sunrise with him. But I turned towards the taxi.

I had an idea then that Freddie saw the law coming and no longer cared, or perhaps that he cared for the ghosts of the past more than he did for those who loved him in the present. If so, that he felt this was some kind of blood price that he was paying, a high price if you ask me, not a price he should have willingly traded for his life, for his songs.

A day later, so I pieced together, the policeman with the brown leather belt reappeared, regretful and determined. The hostel owner stood behind him. He said he'd been informed that a van had driven from Banaras on the Agra Road. One headlamp only was working, sir. Very few Land Rovers went through Uttar Pradesh. The chief eyewitness was certain the driver was a westerner. Could Frederick account for his movements the previous week? The policeman wanted to see the Land Rover and search his possessions. I had imagined all this and seen it coming. I had not reckoned on the search.

The stash wasn't a haul in the grand scheme of things, laughable when you read about the kingpins of Bombay or the pirates who control the waters of the Arabian sea nowadays. Not warehouses or even suitcases. Just a few tawdry bags and tins under the van's seats. More than strictly personal possession – the tolas weighed all on the wrong side. The Delhi Police had been encouraged to make an example of westerners who were bringing their country into disrepute. The previous month there'd been a rumour about LSD in Delhi's water supply. The *Times of India* described hippies as outcastes from their own countries. How does their conduct help the betterment of our society? Their pacifism means nothing except inertia. They are flaunting our customs and conventions. Two separate cases against him, then, 'culpable homicide not amounting to murder', and several charges under the Dangerous Drugs Act. The assumption was that a man had been behind the wheel. Nobody mentioned a passenger.

They towed Vera; a rickety truck came and two young men harnessed her up with rope and chains, spirited her away. There was a blank space outside the guest house for a few days where the van had stood, the road carried the imprint of her undercarriage, until the sand and dirt came on the breeze and the sweepers brushed and blurred the lines and finally her memory was dusted over.

I was back in England by then, in the crisp New Year of 1971, sorting out the deposit on a little flat in Clapham not far, as the crow flies, from the common where I'd first met Fred and Anton. That was my first property, purchased for a song, of course, and soon I had my hands full, painting it and doing up the kitchen. I have to admit I took some pride in arranging my collection of objects in the glass cabinets in the lounge.

I used to like sitting on that sofa, looking at my *objets trouvé*. And often I would relax there among the scatter cushions and read the newspapers. I used to – in those days – go down to Patel's, and collect the Sunday papers, and you can imagine the morning I saw it. The second story, right there on the front page. On every newspaper in the land.

Fred's face on the front of the *Daily Mail*. A golden halo, recognisable, even with a dirty face and a thick beard. They had tied his hands together – and I held up the paper for a long time, trying to work out if they'd used handcuffs or rope. It was hard to tell, the picture wasn't very clear. And he didn't look too bad, considering, not much thinner from what I could tell; I'm sure the stories about the food in those jails are grossly exaggerated. And a shy glance up at the camera, at the journalists clamouring for a story of the earl's drugged-up son. Famous at last, Fred, was my first thought.

I'd known it was coming, I'd suspected they'd find him. He was a fool not to leave when I did. Why didn't he come with me? That was his mistake. We could have made such a different life together. And you might think I could have done something differently in the situation, given all that I've told you about the road, but, really, what could I have done? Should I have gone and spilled the beans, owned up to my part in the whole affair? Turned myself in to the authorities? What good would that have achieved? As far as I was concerned, my overland trip was finished business. Ancient history. I folded that newspaper shut.

Having said that, I was gripped by the story, like many other people in the country. For many days afterwards, I found myself walking down to Patel's and buying up a copy of every single paper, scouring the columns for news. The editors liked his face – it shifted papers – and so we got the ins and outs of the case, his father's arrival in Delhi, and photos outside the Delhi courthouse, all the lawyers flitting in and out like bats. The earl's son gone haywire on the hippie trail, caught with an ingot of hashish. The aristocrat on drugs, a picture of his bowed golden head again, the second time looking a little wilder, darker shadows under his eyes, as if he'd been roughed up, perhaps, and they liked to place it side by side with a photograph from his school days, clean-cut in a blazer, to rub in the point: how the mighty have fallen. I still have all the clippings somewhere.

The defence used every card they could play. Amnesty International said Tihar Jail was one of the worst in the world. Slumdwellers complained to the government because the prison smelled so bad, and it was on record that you could smell it for several kilometres: worse than an open sewer, worse than a rubbish dump, because it stank of all the accumulated shit and sweat and hormones of fifteen thousand unwashed men.

The earl did his best to pull strings, you could see that, reading between the lines, top QCs consulted and all the rest of it but, it turned out, his father's writ didn't run so far anymore. The earl's power had waned. The judge used the occasion for sentencing to take a swipe at all the wasters using India as a playground. He was stern, and said Fred should have known better. Such a privileged young man. The case was a warning to other youth from the west. That was why they sent him down for so long.

It wasn't my place to interfere. I had to look out for myself. I know how to keep my mouth shut. He took the fall for me. I haven't said a word over the years, haven't really thought back on it much at all, actually. The best policy is living in the present. Too many people indulge themselves with navel-gazing, we have to guard against it. I like to think that Fred would have agreed. Wasn't he the one who liked to say, Be Here Now. They all said it in those days and, I've come to understand, it's not a bad message to live by: Be Here Now. And up until now, I've avoided too much self-reflection on those times. It's all old history.

It was never quite clear what happened next. The man who waded into the water, or took one too many bad trips. The back of a man with a pack slung over his shoulder, and a sadness within him which thousands of miles couldn't shake, a hard stone as jagged as a lump of quartz, sitting heavy inside him, perhaps it was shaken loose. Perhaps he found his guru. I liked to think he found a life of peace near the beach, eating good fresh coconut, and swimming far out into the sea. Perhaps he floated with his face to the sky on the surface of the waters. No news, no letters, no one could ever explain where he had gone or what had happened to him once he had been released many years later and was seen boarding a train on the platform at Hazrat Nizamuddin.

Anton said to me once, what are you going to do with your life, once we get back? And you might be wondering how it has worked out for me. I didn't fancy the idea of working for anyone – wanted to be my own boss. In my mind I thought, naively perhaps, a café or a bookshop owner. I knew by the time I came to the end of the overland that I could deal with the divorce papers, that that sorry episode would shrink to a footnote in the long story of my life.

Although if you look at my track record, I haven't exactly been an expert in the relationship department since.

And as it has turned out, antiques have suited me down to the ground. I can't claim to be at the high end, not dealing with the calibre of things that Anton liked. Some people might even call it bric-a-brac. I've got an eye, it turns out, for the things people discard when their loved ones die; plates and china ornaments left behind in house clearances and hurriedly dumped outside charity shops. I drive around car boot sales, fix things up, decide on a price: beaten iron weathervanes, and paintings of cockfights or barber's shops, whirligigs in the shape of soldiers. Some collectors have paid a lot. One American fellow in Connecticut has developed a taste for what he calls English folk art, the prices seem to keep going up. I can't claim to know a lot about everything I sell. It's hard enough to understand the past of your own country, I realise now, and that's why I don't beat myself up about my ignorance back then, on the trail. It's a tall order just to get by, I don't have time for guilt. I am a survivor, you understand.

And recently, there was a car boot sale in the grounds of a large old country house, nicely restored, creamy stone, typical of the eighteenth century, not remarkable. And I hadn't made the connection, hadn't thought. Just put the postcode in the satnav as I do on a Sunday. Rolled up in my car, local lads in fluorescent bibs directing the vehicles into makeshift rows. And then the parking attendant said welcome and the name on their badge went off like a firecracker in my head. Which county was I in? Gloucestershire. All thoughts of buying ornaments gone,

I walked away from the stalls and huddles of people, crunching back up the gravel drive.

The house was open to the public, and I was asked if I wanted a visitor map or an audio guide. I refused both. I was being drawn on like a sleepwalker. Beyond the first room was a hallway with a grand piano and a staircase that swept around like a spiral shell. There were long chintz curtains framing the garden doors, and the dominant colours – yellows and pinks – made the impression unexpectedly feminine, as if the women of the house had taken full charge of the decoration. The doors looked out onto a rose garden. The drawing room was the same, large oriental rugs, and a chaise longue and occasional chairs, another fine piano topped with rows of silver-framed family pictures, flowery notes everywhere. I peered at the photos, some of them black and white – a jazz-age portrait, the young bride in a veil wreathing her head, and the shadows of Fred's face could have been there, among the children in smocks and T-bar shoes, although I couldn't identify him, and the other pictures were surprisingly modern, of a woman in a tightly fitted wedding dress, and others with funny little feathers on their heads that I think they call fascinators, and recent graduation portraits.

A tour group in front of me was chattering with enthusiasm about the house, and I began to feel doubtful, as if I was in the wrong place, as if I'd made an incorrect assumption. Those pictures could have been of any young boys in top hats or sailor suits. The whole overland seemed like a dream and I wondered if it was my own fantasy, if those days in India had never happened. I don't have photographs, no contact with anyone from those days, so, to be honest, it's been easier over the years to think of it all as a strange hallucination that might never have taken place, that might have been a creation of the working of my mind, my mind inventing its own reality. Definitely not something I ever needed to worry about.

I turned left and the tour group peeled away in the other direction. The next room was more weighty, and wood-panelled. The library. Floor-to-ceiling shelves on two sides, with substantial brown spines, some of the shelves locked behind glass. Alone, I approached the writing desk, mahogany with green leather inlay. The desk still looked like it was in daily use under the canopy of a green lamp – or perhaps it was a display? – so there was a pen on the desk which looked as if it had just been used, sheaves of blotting paper splayed out underneath. A pot of Parker ink to the side, balls of scrunched-up paper in the wicker basket, an antique stapler, slightly rusty, a hefty elephant paperweight, black marble, with tusks carved from ivory which had yellowed like old teeth. More framed photographs, a small boy off to school, a trunk almost up to his waist, with letters stencilled on the side spelling out Carruthers. Two boys mucking about in a rowboat on a lake. Shirtless – the absolute agile beauty of those long-limbed boys, looking at each other. I took out my phone and snapped that one, and have it here now in front of me.

I placed my hands on the desk and knew where I was, and the trance had come to an end. I glanced behind me, and sat in the chair for a moment, leaned back against the wooden frame. I imagined the call from this desk from the vintage telephone with its black-and-white rotor and lifted it to my ear, to hear only the silence. A view down to the lake from the window. I could sense Anton's wonder in this library as he was handed a Persian manuscript.

In a shelf of the desk was a stack of blue envelopes, cigarette-paper thin, with red-and-blue airmail stripes. I peered at them, put on my glasses, and the smudged postmarks came into focus. India. A thin stack, not many, perhaps ten – sent over many, many years, all through the years since, that wasn't a lot of contact over five decades. And the handwriting on them, expressive looping with circles for dots. Perhaps a little wilder than I remembered, a little more uneven, but unmistakably his. With a pang I realised that he had never written to me, never tried to make contact, but then, you see, I had never given him my address. He wouldn't have known how to reach me even if he had been desperate to do so, you understand? He might have written me many letters and they just never found me.

The letters were translucent and almost weightless as I picked them up, sliced clean across the top by someone confident with a paperknife. A certain blurred softness to the paper, no longer crisp along the edges, they had been handled and read and refolded many times. Each one addressed to the earl, usually in pencil, once in wacky purple ink. One was in huge and unhinged letters, as if written under the influence. They told me he'd lived a life of hedonism and addiction and disarray, without consistency or pattern, and they told me, most importantly, that he had lived on.

I traced my finger over the ink, lightly, and the paper smelled – perhaps it was only my imagination – of camphor.

I paused and didn't dare unfold the letter, but then I saw, behind them all, remaining in the little ledge of the desk, not an airmail letter but a postcard. A poor-quality postcard which had been left to fade and peel on a stand in the sunlight for many years before being purchased from a village stall; the kind of place where they had given up on ever selling any of those postcards, stamps erratically placed, taking up half of the blank side of the card. Perhaps that's what he'd intended, to have room to say very little. The largest stamp of a crane, drawn in indigo, opening up its wings into flight. Love from Fred. That was all it said. I turned it over. An old postcard from somewhere in the Himalayas, but the photographer had timed it perfectly, so that the very profile of the mountains was edged in rose-pink enamel, softly at first, a song starting up, and then the hard glare of it, the fat yellow sun over the mountains. And every edge, every surface of those mountains, sculpted as if from glass and ice and diamonds. The pinkest sky and the whitest mountains. The rays burnishing each glacier.

That desk belonged to the third earl, Charles Carruthers. He died in the 1980s. He was a lovely man. A great help to the village. A real philanthropist, you know. Very much missed. A volunteer had entered without me noticing and had been watching me. She had assumed the authority of the house, and I pulled away from the desk, posed more casually. I'm afraid those letters that you're holding aren't for manhandling, she said breezily, and watched as I replaced them reluctantly in the shelf of the desk. His daughter insists on keeping his library the same. She can't bear to change a thing.

And in confirmation, when I turned, on the wall to the

east was the portrait, a commanding frame, a man who was Fred and was not Fred. A fair-haired man, in casual clothes rather than uniform, crouching with his dog, in an open-necked shirt. A decent post-war portrait, tastefully done, and the man came out of it well. He looked decisive, the sort of man who would know just what to do in an emergency. His nose florid and neck wide, he didn't have the same delicacy as Fred. His hair was thick and swept to the side. The artist had used the same shades of blue for his eyes and for the sky, behind him stretched the estate, sheep picked out in little flecks of white.

I was doubtful about whether this woman really knew the family's thoughts – she was a local busybody, a village gossip – and she went on to tell me about the daughter – Fred's elder sister, I realised – and her children, and more recently, how wonderful, grandchildren! How the house was thriving, they were experimenting with holiday lets and these antiques fairs, opening the house up on weekends. Her eldest son had been taking more of an interest of late, had decided it was time to step back from the merchant bank, had relocated his family back to the village from London.

She didn't mention Fred. It he had been written out of the family story, the blackest of sheep. I made my excuses and went back through the hallway and round to the exterior of the house. Parts of the house were closed to the public, carefully separated from the visitor areas, so that people – the public, like myself, I suppose – could only go to some rooms, and the heart of the house was secluded, and it was hard to see in through the shaded windows.

Outside, I looked up from the steps which tumbled

down from the great doorway, at the windows which might have been his room, to the vista along to an artificial lake. Georgian windows in long, lovely symmetry, large double doors. Livestock dotted on the field. Everything in place. I could almost see inside, not quite, the gilt frames of the oldest portraits in the hall, Elizabethan ruffs, perhaps, not the pictures inside them, the colour of long window drapes but not behind them. To the other side lay the kitchen, and on that side I encountered a red rope which had been strung from brass rings, a cordon.

On the steps of the house was a child's tricycle lying on its side, abandoned in haste. A water bowl for a family dog. A woman emerged from a side door, a housekeeper, I supposed, brisk and formal, a basket in hand; the smell of baking drifted from inside the house. I'm afraid this part of the house is closed to the public. You are welcome to walk in the grounds. She gestured to a small sign on the lawn which said more or less the same thing, to reinforce her point. And are the family in residence? Well, some of us. We're a large family. I see. I was a little embarrassed at my faux pas. I had mistaken a member of the family for staff. And the earl? Is he here? She was already turning away from me, towards a walled garden. The third earl died a very long time ago. No, I mean his son, the fourth earl, Frederick Carruthers.

Oh, Freddie? She stopped in her tracks and – did I mistake it? It may have been a passing cloud – a blush across her face. Then she looked at me quizzically. The earl is away from home. You won't hear much of him, I'm afraid. He's been away a very long time.

Author Note

Many hundreds of thousands of people, mostly young Americans and Europeans, completed the journey overland from Britain to India in the late 1950s up until the late 1970s. One estimate is that more than a million made the journey from London to India by bus, van, or simply by hitch-hiking during these decades. There were several well-trodden routes, although the journey from Europe almost always went through Turkey, Afghanistan and Pakistan. Companies offered cheap tickets for organised tours by coach and minibus, and travellers set out in old military vehicles, jeeps and even old ambulances. The trail came to an end with the Iranian Revolution which began in 1978, and the Russian invasion of Afghanistan the following year, which made the route from Turkey overland to south Asia much more difficult and dangerous for travellers, if not impassable.

I'm grateful for the published accounts of many old overlanders, mostly unknown to me, who have shared memories of their travels online in recent years in blogs, books and films. Many of these include unique and priceless photographs. In particular I enjoyed the blog and photographs of Richard Gregory, Jean-Claude Latombe's website and photographs, Mark Abley's *Strange Bewildering Time: Istanbul to Kathmandu in the Last Year of the Hippie Trail*, David Shirreff's *Overland 1970*, Ash Lingam's *The Trail to Kathmandu*, and the documentary *Last Hippie Standing* directed by Marcus Robbins. Needless to say, this is a work of fiction.

I have also particularly benefitted from reading *The Hippie Trail: A History* by Sharif Gemie and Brian Ireland (Manchester University Press, 2017), Stuart Hall's 'The Hippies: An American "Moment"' (1968), and Agnieszka Sobocinska's 'Following the "Hippie Sahibs": Colonial Cultures of Travel and the Hippie Trail' published in the *Journal of Colonialism and Colonial History* (2014). Also, numerous works on modern British and imperial history, too many to credit, but particularly *Histories of the Hanged* (2005) by David Anderson.

Above all, I am grateful to all the old travellers I have known personally over the years, some no longer with us, and remember their company with affection.

Acknowledgements

Thank you to Jim Gill, Clare Gordon, Laura Palmer and Madeleine O'Shea for shaping the early days of this book, and Sophie Whitehead, who has been a dedicated and insightful editor throughout; thank you very much, Sophie. Thank you to Louis Greenberg, Simon Michele, Charlie Hiscox, Kate Wands, Amber Garvey, Emily Champion, Shannon Hewitt, Jo Liddiard, Karen Dodds, Dan Groenewald, Victoria Eddison, Kim Yudelowitz and Nikky Ward. My students and colleagues at Oxford, at *History Workshop Journal*, Kellogg College, and other friends and family who have sustained me. Many people I've met along the way, in countries described in this book, and those who welcomed me to their homes. I am very grateful both for generosity abroad, and for those friends in Wallingford who have made it possible to be at home. I remember Rebecca Loncraine, and her book *Skybound* is a continued inspiration. Thank you to my early readers, Judy Cordery, Richard Cordery, Jamie Khan and Alpa Shah, and also Janet Thompson. Preti Taneja made incisive comments at a crucial moment; thank you. Hugh

Armstrong, Sebastian Stride, and Martin Sadler for the stories and music. Amy, Blanche, Stan, Hazel, as ever. And with the deepest gratitude for the constancy of my own travelling companions – Adam, Amira, Leo and Markus.

About the Author

YASMIN CORDERY KHAN is a novelist and historian. She is the author of *The Great Partition, The Raj at War,* and *Edgware Road.* She lives in Oxfordshire.